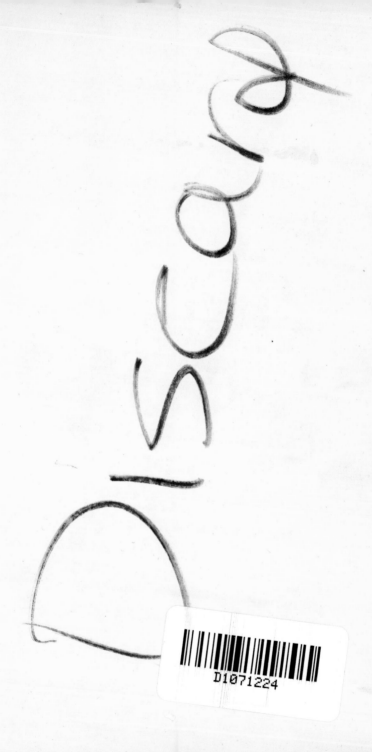

Discard

Drummer Boy for Montcalm

Drummer Boy
for Montcalm

BY WILMA PITCHFORD HAYS

Illustrated by Alan Moyler

New York

THE VIKING PRESS

Fifth printing September 1967
Fic 1. Montcalm-Gozon, Louis Joseph de, Marquis de Saint Veran
2. Quebec Campaign, 1759

PRINTED IN THE U. S. A. BY THE VAIL-BALLOU PRESS, INC.

For
    Peter
    Wallace
    Ellen
    Elda
    Grace
    Wilma
    Grace Ann

Governor Vaudreuil's headquarters

right-flank camp

French

bridge of boats

Canadians & Indians

St. Charles River

British army

French Lines

meadow

Plains of Abraham

Palace Gate
St. John Gate
St. Louis Gate

Landing place

QUEBEC

ST. LAWRENC.

British ships move up
past Quebec
to land Wolfe's men

French fire rafts

Point Lévis

British batteries
and camp

General Monckton's camp

Area of the
Quebec Campaign

Contents

10 CONTENTS

Drummer Boy for Montcalm

Prologue: Rivalry in the New World

By the time the Pilgrims left the *Mayflower* to make their homes at Plymouth the French town of Quebec, in Canada, was already twelve years old.

Samuel de Champlain had explored the St. Lawrence River in 1603, founded Quebec on its northern shore in 1608, and in 1609 discovered the lake named for him, Lake Champlain.

Even before the founding of Quebec, French missionaries had followed the earlier explorer Jacques Cartier to the New World, to live among the Indians and teach them. Later one of these Jesuit priests, Jacques Marquette, joined the trader and explorer Louis Jolliet, and together they sailed up the St. Lawrence River to the Great Lakes. From the Great Lakes they followed the Mississippi River south and proved that this long water highway would help the spread of settlers through the vast New World as far as the Gulf of Mexico.

French settlers came to the New World and called it New France. English settlers called it New England.

For more than a hundred years jealousy grew between the English and the French colonists. Each group believed that the rich furs and land in the New World belonged to *his* country. The English settlers accused the French of stirring up the Indians against them. The French pointed to an equal number of cruel attacks on French settlements by "English-loving" Indians. At last the rivalry for possession of the New World broke out into the French and Indian War. The French were most often victorious in battle, and it looked as if they were going to win.

Their greatest fortress was the walled town of Quebec, built on the rock cliffs near Cape Diamond. Here the French army, commanded by General Louis Joseph de Montcalm, guarded the St. Lawrence River, the gateway into the New World.

In the summer of 1759 England sent a great fleet of ships, heavily armed, bearing thousands of soldiers, sailors, and marines, to make another attempt to capture the French stronghold of Quebec. In command, England sent the clever young General James Wolfe, who was said to have won "battles that couldn't be won."

Both General Montcalm and General Wolfe knew that this was to be a desperate battle. Even the soldiers on both sides realized that if Quebec fell, the English fleet could sail up the St. Lawrence River and capture the French settlements inland. The victor in this war would control the New World. Which was it to be, New France or New England?

I. Stowaway

Peter Demo, standing on the deck of a ship bringing French recruits to Quebec, saw Cape Diamond rising two hundred feet above the river. He turned to the soldier leaning on the rail beside him.

"Philippe," he cried, "can the English be mad enough to think they can capture such a rock?"

Philippe d'Argons smiled at the boy's excitement. "Then you like the look of New France?" he asked. "Is it worth even the backlashes and deck scrubbing?"

Peter could still feel the welts across his shoulders.

He looked at his hands, callused and peeling from old blisters, but he grinned. "What is a flogging, and deck scrubbing, now that I have reached the New World?" he said. "It is even more exciting than the Abbé told me it was."

"You have seen nothing yet," Philippe said. "Wait until we are closer and you can see the town—enclosed by thick stone walls—and, beyond the town, the wilderness. The tallness of the pines here is something to behold."

Peter looked at Philippe. To think that he had actually lived in the wilderness! For several years Philippe d'Argons had been a *coureur de bois*, one of a band of adventurous Frenchmen who roamed the woods and trapped furs when they were not fighting for New France. Recently Philippe had gone back to France to settle the estate of his father. Now he was returning to fight again for Quebec.

Like everyone else on the ship, Peter knew that the walled fortress would soon be attacked. Just before his ship had sailed from France a messenger had raced to the dock with the news. French secret agents had learned that a great armament was being fitted out in English ports to sail for and attack Quebec.

"I wish we were bringing happier news to the

people of Quebec," Philippe said, "but at least we can warn General Montcalm."

Peter saw canoes come from the direction of the town to meet the ship. "Are those pilots to help us through the channel?" he asked.

Philippe nodded.

Peter heard a pilot shout, "*En avant!*—Get under way!"—and slowly the ship moved forward through the zigzag channel of the harbor.

These shoals seem to be dangerous, Peter thought. When the English fleet comes, maybe it will be wrecked here before it can reach Quebec. No French pilot will come out to guide the enemy in!

As Peter and Philippe watched the activity of the ships three young recruits stopped at the rail beside them and asked Philippe about the entrenchments which could be seen along the shore on the right.

"Those are our army camps," Philippe said. "They stretch for six miles along the harbor shore between the Rivers Montmorency and Saint Charles."

"Then the English devils can't land before Quebec," one soldier said with satisfaction.

Peter watched Philippe point out General Montcalm's headquarters to the men and he thought,

Philippe *does* remind me of my father—at least, the way I remember my father before I went to live with the Abbé.

Peter had been very young when he was brought to live with the Abbé. One night his nurse had taken him from his bed and they had driven swiftly through the night in a carriage. In the morning Peter awoke to find himself in Abbé Feron's house.

Peter could remember only snatches of his life before that time. He remembered his mother, who laughed and sang and hugged him often. She had soft brown hair, but his father's hair had been as rusty-black and curly as Peter's own.

His father used to sit at a table in a great room with a dark beamed ceiling. Peter remembered him bent over his papers, with a quill pen in his hand. Sometimes his father would rise and walk back and forth before a curtain of flames in the fireplace. Then he would read aloud the words he had written. And the power of his father's voice sent prickles up and down Peter's spine.

"Your father's voice could stir men," the Abbé had told Peter when the boy grew old enough to understand. "Even his written words fired the common people of France to cry out against the many

injustices they suffer. He wrote of men chained for
life in dungeons because they displeased the king, of
taxes which the court spent on jewels and pleasure
while the people died of starvation. But his words
reached the king and cost your father his life—your
mother's too, since she died of grief."

Peter had looked at the Abbé and felt deeply
moved. "When I am grown," he said, "I shall speak
out as my father did—"

"Enough!" the Abbé had cried, peering uneasily
into the dusk of his garden. "Your head will serve
France best on your shoulders, particularly if you
fill it with knowledge. The world will always need
good men of learning, Peter."

The Abbé meant what he said. For seven years
Peter had to study each day. He learned Latin and
Greek, English and German and Dutch. He studied
history and accounting.

"Store up your fortune in your head," the Abbé
often cautioned the boy. "Then no one can steal it
and you always have it with you."

During the day the Abbé was strict about lessons,
but in the evenings the two often sat before the fireplace in winter or in the walled garden in summer.
Then the old man liked to hear Peter sing. In return the Abbé talked to the boy about many things.

He told Peter of the year he had spent in the New World when he was young.

"The wilderness is savage," he said, "but it is beautiful, and it belongs to no man. Luxurious furs can be trapped in it by anyone willing to work. Perhaps it is the best hope for a young man whose father's estates have been seized by the king." Here the Abbé cleared his throat and blinked hard. "That's something we need not think of until you are much older."

But the Abbé had died suddenly. Peter wept beside his grave, then sobered as he realized that he no longer had a home. He would have to make his own living.

"I am strong and not afraid of work," he said aloud, as if the old man could still hear him. "Somehow I must reach the New World and make my fortune."

Le Bon Dieu—the good Lord—must have heard me, Peter thought, if the Abbé could not. For that very afternoon as the boy walked along the shore of the harbor he saw several ships making ready to sail. He inquired and learned that these were ships for the recruits for the army of General Montcalm at Quebec.

Peter managed to sneak on board a ship and hide

in a roll of sail until the fleet was far at sea. When he was so hungry and thirsty that he was forced to crawl from his hiding place the angry first mate had flogged him with a rope and set him to scrubbing decks for his passage.

Some of the soldiers had laughed to see Peter's awkward attempt to do the hard work he had never done before. But Philippe had spoken to him and that evening poured a healing liquid over Peter's cracked hands. During the long voyage the man and the boy had become friends.

Although Philippe d'Argons said little about himself, Peter saw that the officers on board the ship respected him. And Peter knew that many adventurous gentlemen chose the freedom of the New World rather than live in France under the selfish, lazy King Louis.

II. There Is Quebec

The sun scattered a mist that frosted the river, and the ship nosed its way to the dock.

"There is Quebec," Philippe said.

Peter knew there was no use trying to speak when his heart was thumping so fast and his eyes were so busy trying to see everything. Quebec seemed to be two towns. The Lower Town, a string of shops and warehouses, a church and a market square, crowded close together on a narrow strip of beach between the river and the rock cliff. Perched on the cliff above was the Upper Town, enclosed in massive stone walls. Peter could see that the rock mountain was covered with buildings, and not one building seemed to be on a level with another. He saw churches and gardens and slate-roofed houses with dormer windows, like the houses he had known in France. A great stone palace overlooked the Lower

Town. Above it fluttered the white flag of France. Peter felt his throat tighten.

"You were not expecting anything as grand as our governor's palace, the Château Saint Louis?" Philippe asked. "Also, see the turrets across the town, above the Saint Charles River? That is the palace of the intendant. These two govern Quebec and all New France."

Peter looked puzzled. "I thought General Montcalm was in charge here during the war," he said.

Philippe's mouth hardened. "If he were we'd have a better chance against the English fleet," he said. "Governor Vaudreuil is jealous of Montcalm and does everything he can to embarrass the general. The intendant, Bigot, is worse. He—"

The ship jarred against the wharf. Peter forgot his interest in whatever it was that made the intendant, Bigot, worse than the jealous governor. Everyone from Quebec and the surrounding countryside seemed to be here to meet the ships from their home country. Those who had not already arrived were hurrying down a steep winding path from the Upper Town to the Lower Town. From the rivers, canoemen and *voyageurs*—boatmen of the big barge-like *bateaux*—were making their way toward shore.

Sailors in red caps and sashes called to girls who

ran to meet them. A bearded habitant stood at the water's edge and played his fiddle as if he expected the people to break into song and to dance upon the pebbly beach. Peter recognized the tune and sang a few words lustily, waving at the old fiddler.

Oh, he had been right to come! This exciting New World was the place for him!

Peter crowded down the gangplank behind Philippe, who was having trouble protecting a package he carried under one arm.

"Wait here for me," Philippe said when they reached the beach. "I must send warning of the English attack to my commander, the Chevalier de Ramezay. Then we'll go to the home of Grandpère Bonheur, as I told you."

Peter stood on the wharf among chattering, pushing people. He saw porters begin to roll barrels and chests from the ships. Each chest was marked for the same owner, the Grand Company of Associates. More porters came to carry the chests to a great warehouse near the beach.

Peter noticed two men standing at the open door of the warehouse, inspecting the cargo as the porters entered. One, short and dark, wore fine velvet breeches and jacket with lace at the wide sleeves. Peter decided he must be a prosperous merchant.

Perhaps he is one of the associates of the grand company that owns so much, Peter thought. If only he might need a strong boy to work for him!

Peter had no money, and no clothes except what he was wearing when he stowed away on the ship. Philippe had invited him to go along to deliver a package to his friends, Grandpère and Marie Bonheur, from their relatives in France, and had said that Marie would surely have a good dinner ready for them. After that Peter did not know what he would do.

He planned eventually to go into the wilderness for furs, but there was the matter of traps and food. These cost money. He must have a job.

He walked toward the two men beside the warehouse door. "*Pardon*," he said to the short dark man with a blotched skin. "I would like to work for such a prosperous organization as the Grand Company of Associates."

Both men turned. Peter held out his arm and flexed his muscles. "I am strong," he said. "I have scrubbed decks." The second man hunched his heavy shoulders and a scowl puckered his full-moon face. "And after lessons," Peter added hastily, "I hoed in the garden and chopped wood for the Abbé."

"We've enough porters," the moon-faced man growled. "Now get out—"

"Wait," the man in the gentleman's clothes said. "You said lessons. Can you count and read and write a little? These skills are not easy to find."

Peter's face lighted. The Abbé had been right: the knowledge he carried in his head was always with him. "*Oui*, I read and write and count," he said. "And—"

Before Peter could add that he understood several languages, the man said, "Then we can use you in the warehouse as a counting boy. Report first thing in the morning." Peter saw him wink at his surly, moon-faced companion. "We must keep a careful tally for the minister of war in France, who is always screaming that he sends more supplies than we receive—eh, Cadet?"

The moon-faced Cadet seemed almost to smile, thought better of it, then growled at Peter. "See that you're here at sunup."

"*Oui*, I'll be here," Peter promised.

He saw Philippe returning and ran to meet him. "Not a half-hour in the New World," Peter boasted, "and I have work."

Philippe's dark brows lifted and he smiled. "Carrying baskets up Mountain Hill Road, I suppose, for

a gentlewoman who admired the length of your eye-
lashes?" he teased.

"I am counting boy in the warehouse of the
Grand Company of Associates," Peter said. "I was
hired by those two—standing at the door."

Philippe stared. "The intendant, Bigot, and his
butcher accomplice, Cadet," he said in such astonishment that Peter grinned.

"This is better than anything I could hope for!"
Philippe said. He seemed so excited that Peter was puzzled. Philippe took the boy's arm and started toward
the narrow winding path that led up the cliff to the
Upper Town. "Peter," he said earnestly, "try to remember the final count of chests each day, and we
will keep a record for General Montcalm. Then he
can know how many of the supplies from France
actually reach him."

"What do you mean?" Peter asked.

"Bigot has charge of all supplies for the army,
even all supplies for the people," Philippe said.
"Farmers must sell their grain to him; trappers must
sell him their furs. He is supposed to send the furs
to France to help pay for war supplies, and to dis-
tribute the grain among the people and the army.
But he sells secretly to the *Hollandais*—the Dutch

on the Hudson River—even to the English, and puts the gold in his own pocket."

Peter, bending forward to climb Mountain Hill Road, felt the hair on the back of his neck prickle. He was going to work for such a man. "Why isn't Bigot reported?" he asked. "Surely the governor—"

"Bigot is too powerful. He is responsible for the transportation of all troops, of both men and supplies. General Montcalm must depend upon his cooperation. The general can't even report him to the minister of France, since Bigot has a powerful friend in the court. He's a favorite of the Marquise de Pompadour."

Peter nodded. All France knew that La Pompadour led the king by the nose.

"But if General Montcalm had definite proof to send to France, even La Pompadour could not save Bigot," Philippe continued. "Are you willing to keep your eyes open, Peter? It is dangerous, if Bigot or Cadet discovers what you are doing. But it is something you can do for France."

Peter felt his cheeks grow warm. He was too young for the army, but he loved his country. "You can trust me," he promised. "I will keep careful count."

They had passed through the narrow streets to the back of the town where houses sat on little terraces overlooking the St. Charles River. Philippe turned up the cobbled walk to one of these homes where a rosebush climbed beside the front door.

"Here is the home of Grandpère Bonheur and his granddaughter, Marie," Philippe said. "Marie is about your age—and one of the best cooks in Quebec, as you shall see."

III. *La Friponne*

Philippe knocked on the door. Peter heard the sound of running feet. The door burst open and he saw a girl a little shorter than he, with dark curly hair hanging loose to her shoulders, and eyes as blue as the iris in the Abbé's garden.

"Philippe!" she cried. "We wanted to meet the ships, but Grandpère is not so well today—his gout, you know." She saw Peter and smiled at him.

"Marie, this is my friend, Peter Demo," Philippe said.

"Are you straight from France too?" Marie asked.

"Come in, please. Grandpère has been counting the minutes until you came with the news. Did you see Aunt Rose in Paris—and my cousin Michelle?"

Philippe laughed and handed her the package from under his arm. "I think Grandpère is not the only one who has counted the minutes," he said. "Yes, I saw your Aunt Rose. She sent this package to you."

"Grandpère, see what Aunt Rose has sent us!" Marie said, running to the old man who sat in a chair before glowing coals in the fireplace.

Peter saw that he was a big man, stooped, with very white hair. His snowy mustache was neatly combed and trimmed. He chuckled as the girl began to tear open the package she had placed across his knees.

"Come, Philippe, my friend," the old man said. "And the boy too. Marie will remember her manners in a moment and ask you to be seated."

Peter saw that Marie had taken two dresses from the package. Her eyes sparkled as she held one to each shoulder, a red dress and a blue dress, both made of some silky soft stuff.

At least something can make her speechless, Peter told himself. But where would anyone wear such fine dresses in a wilderness country?

Then Peter realized that this room might have been in a pleasant home in France. From the mantel a china shepherd and shepherdess smiled down upon a red velvet sofa. Near the garden window a round table was covered with a white linen cloth and set with silver candlesticks and sparkling glass. Fine china was laid for dining.

"You are surprised to find us living like civilized beings in this New World?" Grandpère Bonheur asked.

Peter flushed, realizing that he had been staring. "I don't know what I expected, sir," he said.

"We do not forget that we are Frenchmen," the old man said, "and that beauty and order make life worth living. . . . Now tell us of France. How is the war going there? Did the king send the troops and supplies we need so much?"

"Not nearly enough for our battle with the English," Philippe said.

"Oh," Marie cried, "I almost forgot the chicken! I hope it is not too brown."

Peter sniffed the odor of roasting chicken and drew in a deep breath. A few minutes later, when they were all seated at the table, he ate so much that he was almost ashamed to take a third helping of chicken and wild-rice stuffing, but he did.

Then Marie brought little hot biscuits and wild strawberry conserve for dessert. Peter groaned. "Why didn't you tell me there was more to come?" he said. "Food was not like this on the ship of recruits!"

Marie smiled and placed the basket of biscuits in front of him. "You are too young for the army, Peter," she said. "Why did you come to Quebec?"

"To make my fortune in furs," Peter said. "But first I must work to earn the money for traps. I already have a job—counting boy for the Grand Company of Associates."

At the sudden silence Peter looked from Marie's face to her grandfather's. Both had changed instantly, as if his hosts had discovered a snake at their table.

"*You* are going to work for *La Friponne?*" Marie asked.

The angry color left Grandpère Bonheur's face. "Marie, *ma chérie,* the boy could not know." He turned to Peter. "We call the Grand Company 'La Friponne'—The Cheat. Bigot forces the hardworking farmers to sell their grain to La Friponne for a fixed low price. Then he sells it back to the people through his stores at five or six times the price —and those who can't pay can starve."

"Bigot forces the trappers to sell all their furs to the Grand Company," Marie added. "He pretends his law is to help France win the war—so the loyal habitants and coureurs de bois sell for barely enough to live on—then La Friponne sells their furs for its own profit—to the Dutch and English. Bigot's boats sneak them from the warehouse down the river at night, so there will be no proof for the king."

Peter looked at Philippe, who made a movement with his hands and shoulders. Bigot and the men of his Grand Company must be powerful indeed if the people of Quebec knew what he was up to yet had no way of stopping him. Perhaps he should think twice before going to work for such a man.

Philippe rose and made a little bow to Marie. "On the long voyage I thought of this good dinner," he said, "and it was all that I expected it to be. Now we must go—and find a place for Peter to stay."

When they were in the street and walking toward the town Philippe looked down at Peter. "Well?" he said.

Peter knew that Philippe was asking if he could still count on him to keep his eyes open at the warehouse, for proof that Bigot was selling supplies and furs belonging to France. Peter liked Marie and her grandfather. He wanted to be their friend. He remembered the way they had looked at him when he said he was going to work for La Friponne. Surely there must be other jobs a boy could do.

He glanced sideways at Philippe's face, then shrugged. There were some things a person had to do, no matter who disliked him for it. "I'll be at the warehouse at sunup," he said.

Philippe clapped him on the shoulder. "Then you'd better get to bed. I'll speak to the innkeeper at the Fleur de Lys, where I'll live until I go on duty at the town garrison. He'll trust you for food and a bed in the loft."

IV. The Affair of the Furs

The next morning Peter walked along the river, excited by the beehive activity on the wharf. Men swarmed everywhere, unloading ships and storing goods in the warehouse. Beyond were market stalls where people waited, even at this early hour, anxious to buy the goods brought from France.

Peter saw men and women of the town, soldiers from the army camps, even a few Indians. A bateau rowed by coureurs de bois dressed in furs and deerskin tied up at the wharf before the warehouse. The coureurs de bois tossed bundles of furs onto the wharf and leaped after them.

Peter had never seen furs from a trapper's winter catch. He ran toward the bateau, but stopped when he heard a shout behind him. He turned to see Cadet lumbering to meet the coureurs de bois.

"Your work is inside," he said, scowling at Peter. "Report to the manager."

Peter hoped the manager would place him in that part of the warehouse where he saw the furs being stored, but he was put to work checking produce brought in by the farmers. He recorded hundreds of fat geese and ducks dressed for market, dozens of homemade cheeses and clumps of wild ginseng roots dug in the forest.

After a week of checking these Peter despaired of learning anything that would be helpful to Philippe. Then one afternoon two men entered the counting house and looked about. They were big men with coarse beards and shoulder-length blond hair. They approached Peter.

"We have come to see Monsieur Cadet," one of them said in halting French with a strong Dutch accent.

These men must be Hollandais, Peter thought. They may even be two of the Dutch who buy furs illegally from La Friponne. I must keep my wits about me. "All the Grand Company is meeting today at the intendant's palace, for a council of dividends," he said.

The older Hollandais winked at the other and spoke in his own language. "When the cat is away, the mice will play," he said. "While Montcalm visits

the Indian camps, Bigot and Cadet divide their profits
—and send for us to buy the furs they cheated the
Indians out of—before Montcalm returns."

The younger Hollandais nodded. "When Montcalm returns and goes to the governor to demand
that Bigot return the Indian furs, there'll be no furs
here."

They would not say so much, Peter thought, if
they knew I understood them. I must try to keep on
their trail until I can report to Philippe.

"Tonight, after the dividend meeting, there will
be a great party at the intendant's palace," Peter
went on. "All the townspeople are invited to come
into the balcony and look down upon the dining and
dancing in the ballroom. You will be welcome there
—and they say Bigot feeds every person as well as he
does the noble guests."

The Hollandais laughed and slapped their thighs.
"I told you this Bigot knew how to keep the habitants in line," the older man said. "With one hand
he steals from them; with the other he offers them
hospitality, music, and food. Then they think Bigot
must be a good fellow and that the tales told about
him are false!"

"I've heard of his parties," the other said. "There's

gambling below in the kitchens—and the food and wine are the best. Let's get our share of the Grand Company's dividends at the card table."

"These French are good at cards," the older Hollandais warned as they walked away.

Peter could scarcely keep his mind on his work until the end of the day. He ran all the way to the Fleur de Lys, but Philippe was not in his room or in the tavern below. A maid said she thought that he had gone to the party at the intendant's palace.

It was dusk by the time Peter reached the palace. He stood before the expanse of massive stone, topped by turrets and towers. Windows were lighted high and low. He could hear the music of violins, laughter, and singing. He looked down at his worn jacket and breeches and at his cracked shoes. He could not go to the balcony dressed like this. He would try the kitchen first.

He walked around the palace through terraces of gardens until he reached the kitchen door. As he pushed it open, odors of roasting fowl and meat drew him quickly inside. One of the servant girls, carrying a platter of stuffed piglets, stopped abruptly to avoid bumping into him.

"What are you doing in the kitchen?" she cried. "One your age has no business here."

A red-cheeked woman at the fireplace turned from the kettle of savory soup she was stirring. Peter swallowed and smiled. She winked. "What is any boy doing in a kitchen?" she said. "He is hungry. Let him stay." She filled a bowl with hot soup and handed it to Peter.

"*Merci beaucoup*—thank you very much," he said. While he drank the good soup he looked about him.

Across the room he saw men in rough clothing gathered about tables lighted with candles. Some were eating. Some were playing cards intently. Others lounged against the stone wall and watched. At one table everyone was so quiet that Peter knew that the game must have been going on for some time and that the tension was high. He joined the watching sailors and woodsmen and scanned the faces in the dim light to see if Philippe was among them.

Then he saw that two of the men in the tense game were the Hollandais. They were gambling with two coureurs de bois who must have come that day from their winter's trapping, since packs of furs were piled beside their chairs.

All the coins were stacked in front of the Hollandais. The faces of the coureurs de bois were flushed with too much wine. Their hands came down heavily on the table.

"We have no more gold," one of them said.

"You have furs," the younger Hollandais said. "Bet them. You may win back your gold."

"Never," one of the coureurs de bois said, throwing his arm over the bundle by his side. "We like to died for these furs. We starved and froze eight months in the northwest regions, but we brought back ermine."

"Ermine fit to trim the robes of the king—or La Pompadour herself," the other coureur de bois boasted. "And otter skins and black and silver fox. We have beaver so soft that the proudest beauty would pay a fortune for it."

"Maybe a beauty would," an onlooker cried, "but you'll get no fortune from La Friponne—scarcely enough to pay for the bait in your traps!"

Peter saw the eyes of the Hollandais glitter, but they pretended not to believe the coureurs de bois' boasts.

"A few mangy beaver," one said to the other. "Maybe this trapper thinks *we* do not *know* fine furs!"

The face of the coureur de bois grew dark with anger. "We will show you fine furs!" he shouted.

From his sash he jerked a hunting knife and cut the leather thongs which bound one bundle. The furs burst from the pack and spilled upon the floor and the table. Peter gasped. He had not dreamed that furs could be as thick and glossy and richly marked as these.

Peter saw greed in the light blue eyes of the Hollandais. Their fingers twitched as they reached to touch a skin. Finally one said, "We will buy your furs—and pay gold."

"How much?" the coureur de bois asked, leaning forward.

A hand came down upon the shoulder of the coureur de bois. Peter saw that it was Philippe's. He must have come into the kitchen during the quarrel.

"My friend, you forget the law," Philippe said to the coureur de bois. "We can sell only to the king's representatives, the Grand Company, no matter how little the price it pays. Do you wish a heavy fine—and to spend the summer in prison?"

For a moment Peter thought the coureur de bois was going to drive his knife into Philippe's stomach. Then his face lighted. "Philippe," he cried, "I did not know you were home! How we missed you this winter!"

The Hollandais scooped the coins from the table

into their big hands and stalked from the room.

Peter took a rich brown pelt from the table and stroked the silky fur. "What animal's fur is this?" he asked.

"Listen to the boy," one of the woodsmen said. "He does not know when he holds the king of Canada in his hands."

Men laughed and Peter's cheeks burned.

"If one keeps his mouth shut, he does not betray his ignorance," a soldier advised.

"If I don't ask, I won't learn," Peter said. "I want to know about furs."

Philippe smiled at him. "This fur is beaver," he said. "Beaver is called king here because there are so many of them and their pelts are very valuable. And in the wilderness we eat beaver meat. The bishop even allows us to eat beaver tail in place of fish on meatless days, if fish can't be had."

"Its *tail?*" Peter said in astonishment.

"Beaver tail is not like the rat's tail," Philippe said, laughing. "Beaver tail is thick and broad and can be boiled. It tastes a little like tallow, but one can live on it."

"Do you often have to eat such food when you are trapping?" Peter asked.

"One gets used to it," Philippe said cheerfully. He

took up another fur from the table. "This pelt is from a fat winter beaver. See how thick and heavy the fur is, how long the guard hairs? The winter beaver's fur is worth much more than that of the summer beaver, which is dry and thin-haired. There are also different grades of summer and winter beaver, old skins and young skins, those which have been tanned properly and those which have had so little care that they are wormy."

"I didn't know there was so much to learn, to be a trapper," Peter said thoughtfully.

A group of coureurs de bois gathered about Philippe and slapped him on the back to welcome him back.

A woodsman sitting near Peter nudged the boy with his elbow. "He didn't tell you about the real king of the forest," he said. "The real king is a little black animal about the size of a pussycat, with white stripes down its back."

Peter looked at him doubtfully.

The woodsman appealed to the other men. "Isn't it true that the small black one with the white stripe down his back is the real king of the forest?" he asked. "Does not every other animal get out of his way when *he* comes down a trail?"

"*Oui*, that is true," the men chorused.

Peter looked from one bearded face to the other. He believed they were teasing him. Still, they could be telling the truth. There was much that was strange in this new world.

Suddenly he remembered why he had come to the palace. He had been so interested in the furs that he had forgotten to report to Philippe about the Hollandais. As he turned to find his friend, he heard a roar of laughter behind him from the sailors and woodsmen.

Peter made his way through the group of coureurs de bois around Philippe and waited for his chance to speak. "Come outside," he whispered. "I have something to tell you."

When they were in the darkness of the garden Peter told all that he had heard the Hollandais say that afternoon at La Friponne.

"What did they mean about Bigot and Cadet cheating the Indians?" Peter ended.

"I'm not sure," Philippe said. "The Indians are not French subjects. They are free to sell to anyone, even the Dutch. They don't have to take the low prices La Friponne pays."

"Then how could La Friponne cheat them?" Peter asked.

"I'm trying to figure that out," Philippe answered.

"I know Bigot delivered the chests of blankets and guns which our ships brought from France for the Indians. But those were gifts, already paid for by the government in France, who agreed to supply the Indians with the things they need while they fight with us—just as it supplies our own army."

"Is that why General Montcalm is visiting the Indian camps now?" Peter asked.

"Yes," Philippe said, "and as soon as he heard that the English fleet was coming he sent couriers to call a meeting of the chiefs of many tribes. He wants to make sure we can count on the Indians' help. He knows this battle with the English will be a desperate one, and we're short of men and supplies."

"Where are the Indian camps?" Peter asked.

"In the wilderness, upriver a few miles," Philippe replied.

He sounded so thoughtful that Peter was silent, although his mind seethed with more questions. How had the Indians been cheated of their furs? Did they know they had been cheated? Did Montcalm know? What did the Hollandais have to do with it?

"Peter," Philippe said, "if Bigot has been cheating the Indians out of their furs it could mean trouble for General Montcalm. They might go back to their homes in anger and refuse to help. I must get together some of the coureurs de bois and go to the camps tonight."

"Let me go with you," Peter said. "Tomorrow's Sunday. I don't have to work."

Philippe hesitated. "No," he said. "We may run into trouble. You've already helped—maybe more than we know. Now get some sleep."

V. King of the Forest

Peter woke to hear the bells of the churches ringing
—deep tones from the little church in the Lower
Town, Notre-Dame de la Victoire; silvery tones
from the beautiful Ursuline convent chapel in the
Upper Town. The musical sounds pleased him and
he lay listening. A beam of sunshine from a small
window under the slate roof warmed his cheek. The
window was open, and he sniffed the warm summer air. His first day free of work in the New
World! He could do as he chose, visit friends or

explore the wilderness outside the stone walls of the town.

Marie and Grandpère Bonheur were the only people he knew, and he did not believe they would welcome him, since he worked for La Friponne. . . .

Suddenly he sat bolt upright. Philippe had said the Indian camp was a few miles upriver in the forest. He would walk in that direction. If he didn't come upon it, at least he could explore the wilderness for the first time.

Peter left the town through the St. Louis Gate. He climbed a long slope to the heights overlooking the St. Lawrence River and stood on a plateau called the Plains of Abraham. He saw that it was a rough rectangle, less than a mile wide, between the cliffs of the St. Lawrence on one side and the valley of the St. Charles River on the other. It stretched more than a mile, dotted with cornfields and trees, and ended in a ridge.

Peter walked the length of the Plains of Abraham and climbed the ridge. Beyond was a sloping hill leading to the banks of St. Denis Brook, which cut through the cliffs and emptied into the St. Lawrence. The banks of the brook were barricaded with fallen trees and brush to keep an enemy from climbing the slope and gaining the Plains. Ahead of him

Peter saw a dozen tents and a few soldiers on guard. This must be the outpost Anse du Foulon of which he had heard.

Peter looked down the sheer drop of cliffs into the water of the mighty St. Lawrence far below, and he smiled.

The English are not flies that they can climb these rocks, he said to himself. Besides, General Montcalm will never let them get above our batteries at Quebec.

Beyond the Plains he saw deep forest and a break in the trees that seemed to be the entrance to a trail. He left the Plains and followed the narrow winding passage. The brown pine needles had been trampled flat. Occasional broken branches from the giant pines and spruce cleared a trail wider than his arms could stretch on either side.

Heavy green boughs grew so thick overhead that the sun came through only in small patterns of light on the dark shadows beneath. It was colder here. Peter shivered and folded his arms across his chest to warm himself.

After a while the passage grew even narrower, the light beneath the trees more like twilight. He whistled and broke into song to give himself courage. But his voice sounded startlingly strange, and he stopped to look about him. He hoped this was the trail to the Indian camp. He had seen no other.

Standing motionless on the path, Peter felt a deep silence about him. Then a kind of music began, as if the wind were playing a tune of its own through a harp made of the high branches of the giant pines and the lower boughs of the spruce. Now it formed a two-part chant so full of rhythm and beauty that Peter felt his eyes sting. Goose bumps prickled on his bare arms. He yearned to capture and put away in his memory this strange song of the forest.

I am not afraid, he thought. I have lived all my life in the most civilized country of the world, yet I love this wilderness.

For the first time the last pang of homesickness left him. The forest's freedom and peace seemed more soothing than anything he had ever known. He smiled. This New France was a great, wild, exciting place, yet he felt at home here.

He was about to walk on, when he heard a soft sound, no more than a stirring of leaves. Coming down the trail toward him was a small animal. Its plume of tail arched gracefully over its back, like a pussycat's. Peter stared. The small animal was black, with white stripes down its back.

Until that moment he had believed that the men in the kitchen of the intendant's palace were teasing him. But they had told the truth. There *was* such an animal as they described. It walked proudly, like a king, moving not an inch to the side of the trail.

Peter stood motionless and watched it approach. His heart began to pound. What a prize, if he could take the fur of this small king of the forest!

Slowly and sedately it came nearer and nearer. Peter could scarcely breathe. Perhaps if he waited until it reached him, he could pounce upon it and capture it with his bare hands.

It stopped a few feet from him and lifted its sharp nose as if surprised that he did not step out of the way. Now was the time—yet is was such a pretty, defenseless creature that Peter hesitated.

I must start to make my fortune sometime, and I may not meet one of these kings again, he thought. He leaped suddenly and felt the fur of the small animal slide through his fingers. Then he was overcome by an odor so shocking that he scrambled to his feet.

Gasping, with both hands cupped over his mouth and nose, he ran into the forest. He lost the trail and plunged against a tree. The odor was here too. He stumbled about, found the trail again, and ran swiftly until pain filled his chest and he gasped for breath. He stopped and leaned against a tree.

Even here the odor followed him. Strong and sickening, it seemed to be everywhere; he could not leave it behind. His clothing reeked from the small creature's spray. He knew now why the men had laughed when they told him about the real king of the forest!

He removed his jacket and held it at arm's length as he followed the trail. Still the odor gagged him. At last he came to a narrow river. He stripped off his clothes and left them on the bank. Standing in the icy water above his waist, he scrubbed his body with his palms and ducked his head in the stream and rubbed his hair.

He came from the water and stood on the riverbank, his teeth chattering. His clothes still reeked. He must wash them and wear them wet.

Peter again waded into the river, carrying his clothes. As he bent to scrub them, he heard laughter and voices. He sat down on the riverbed, with the water up to his shoulders, grateful for his wet clothes ballooning about him in the clear water.

Around a bend in the river floated a small canoe with two Indian boys in it. Three Indian girls swam alongside. They laughed and caught the canoe and turned it over, spilling the boys into the water.

The Indian boys swam as swiftly as slender fish and caught the girls' ankles and pulled them under. The girls surfaced and shook their dripping black hair and shrieked with laughter.

Peter was so astonished to see "savage" children playing games that he forgot his own predicament until one of the girls saw him and pointed and cried, "*Awanock! Awanock!*—White man! White man!"

The children gathered together behind the canoe and swam away, pushing it upstream.

When Peter was sure the children were gone he began to wash his clothes again. Finally he laid them on the bank to dry, but the odor still clung. Back he went into the water. While he was scrubbing he heard a twig snap and turned to see a young Indian standing by the river's edge.

The Indian was half a head taller than Peter, probably several years older. He held one hand over his mouth as if he did not want to hurt Peter's feelings by laughing but could not help himself.

"You have met Monsieur Skunk, the scented weasel," he said in French, and smiled as if he enjoyed Peter's amazement at hearing a savage speak the French language.

Peter saw that the Indian's straight black hair was held back by an embroidered band of doeskin. His fringed hunting shirt of doeskin and his moccasins were beautifully embroidered.

"Your clothes will need to be scrubbed with sand and rubbed with sweet fern and balsam," he said to Peter. "Come, I will take you to my village." The Indian stripped off his knee-length hunting shirt and stood in his loincloth and leggings. Peter came from the river and the Indian pulled the shirt over Peter's head.

"*Merci beaucoup*," Peter said. He picked up his shoes and turned them in his hand. They could not be saved. They were worn and cracked and already too tight for him. Scrubbing would shrink them beyond use. He tossed them into the river to get rid of their odor.

He saw that the Indian was taking off his moccasins. He motioned Peter to sit down on a fallen tree trunk.

Peter protested. "You must not give me your shoes."

"Among my people our mothers teach us these little good things," the Indian boy said quietly. "To feed the hungry and give help to the stranger."

Peter sat down. The Indian lifted Peter's feet and placed the soft doeskin moccasins upon them.

"*Merci beaucoup*," Peter said. "I almost forgot. I am Peter Demo—not long from France."

"I am Bomazeen of the Abnaki'," the Indian said. "Come with me."

VI. Bomazeen of the Abnaki'

"Are you hungry?" Bomazeen asked as Peter followed him along the spongy path on the river's bank. "There is much cooking in our camp. Montcalm, our father from across the waters, is holding council here with the chiefs of many tribes."

Peter felt good to know he had come to the right place. He grinned at the thought of Philippe's face when he saw him.

"Great trouble is coming," Bomazeen said gravely. "Our white father received a message that many English ships are on the water."

"I know," Peter said.

"Our white father spoke the warning before the council broke up to eat. Soon the chiefs will assemble again and decide who will fight for France."

"Can we hear them?" Peter asked.

"Anyone may listen to the council of chiefs,"

Bomazeen said. "And any Indian may speak his
thoughts."

Peter thought of France, where the Notables, who
should have been helping to govern the country, had
not been allowed to meet in more than a hundred
years; where his own father had been put to death
because he spoke and wrote against the king's unjust
laws.

The boys came out of the trees onto the edge of
a clearing along the stream. Peter saw small bark
cabins clustered about a central courtyard paved
with stones. At outdoor fireplaces in the yard Indian
women and girls were cooking and chattering happily.

"Wait here," Bomazeen said. "I will take your
clothes to the women to be washed, and bring you
food."

All along the riverbank Peter saw graceful small
canoes and large sturdy bateaux tied at the water's
edge. On shore the Indian camp resembled a human
anthill. There seemed to Peter to be hundreds of Indians, maybe thousands. Some had painted signs upon
their faces. Some had adorned their heads with scalplock or plumes or buffalo horns. Among the Indians
Peter saw the white uniforms of French officers, the
blue uniforms of French soldiers, and the red toques
of voyageurs, the boatmen of the bateaux. He saw a

black-robed French missionary talking to several coureurs de bois. He tried to see if one of these was Philippe, but they were too far away.

Bomazeen appeared suddenly beside him and Peter started. He smiled, a little embarrassed as the Indian grinned and handed him a bowl of meat stew and a flat corn cake. Over his arm Bomazeen carried leggings for Peter.

"*Merci beaucoup*," Peter said. "I am jumpy, seeing so many strange men with weapons. All the Indians in the New World must be here."

Bomazeen frowned. "Not the English-loving Mohawks," he said. "They fight with the English rangers. But there are chieftains here from forty-nine tribes. They have come from the north, even from the far west, and brought their interpreters with them." He pointed to white men and half-breeds accompanying the chiefs.

Peter thought these interpreters looked as wild and fierce as any Indian there.

"Like white men, Indian tribes speak different languages," Bomazeen explained. "My own people, the Abnaki', speak the Algonquian tongue. Many of us also understand French. We learned it from the missionaries who live with us and from the coureurs de bois who trap with us."

"Do you know the coureur de bois Philippe d'Argons?" Peter asked.

"Who does not?" Bomazeen answered. "He is here. He came by bateau in the night."

"Can we find him—among these thousands?" Peter asked.

"Later," Bomazeen said. "See, our chiefs gather again in council. We must hurry if you want to hear their words."

Peter wiped the corn-cake crumbs from his mouth and pulled on his leggings. The two boys ran across the clearing to the far edge of the forest and sat down behind a throng of men seated cross-legged upon the grass.

Facing a semicircle of silent chiefs stood a Frenchman in such a splendid white and gold uniform that Peter knew he must be General Montcalm. He was about forty-five, slender, not as tall as most of the men there. Peter thought he looked every inch the noble marquis that he was, yet General Montcalm spoke to these proud chiefs as if they were brothers and friends. Peter felt his heart beat faster as he listened to the rapid, fiery speech of the general to whom France owed so much.

"In the forest no one equals your cunning," General Montcalm told the Indians. "You have taught the Canadian habitants your manner of fighting. With you and the Canadians in the woods, with France's cavalry and soldiers upon the plains, the enemy is lost. I give you my solemn word that if we all remain together we shall destroy the English."

"Listen now," Bomazeen whispered. "The Old One is rising. He is chief of the Ottawas and very wise. I will tell you what he is saying."

Excitement raced down Peter's spine as the old Indian began to speak. He had never known any nobleman of France to move with more dignity or choose his words more carefully than this old chief.

"Our father who came from across the sea to help us defend our homeland from the English, your words are good. I, who have seen more moons than anyone here, approve them. The manitou of war has inspired you. The Ottawas will join your fight. We have spoken."

The interpreters turned to each chief and repeated the old one's speech. Most of the Indians clapped. But Peter saw that a dozen chiefs, carrying bow and arrow and hatchets rather than French muskets, scowled and were silent.

Montcalm bowed toward the Old One who had spoken. "I am delighted that the Ottawas, mighty hunters, are with us."

The tallest of the Indian chiefs stood.

"Chief of the Abnaki', my own tribe," Bomazeen said proudly.

"The English treated us as wild wolves," the Abnaki chief said quietly. "From the beginning they hunted us in our forests. They crowded us from our homelands as they crowded the deer. From the beginning of time we, the dawn people, lived in the land of the moose and about the placid lake you call Champlain. The English drove us to the north. The English seeded hatred in our hearts and treachery in our hands.

"But the men of France have treated us as hosts and brothers. They live among us, walk the trails of the forest with us. They marry our daughters and eat and sing with us. They mourn, with us, for our sons who do not return from battle.

"We are bound with our French brothers by solemn ties. Let us take care that these shall not be broken."

Peter was so moved by the dignified musical tones of the Abnaki chief that he sat as if a spell had been cast upon him. Bomazeen repeated the words in French. Peter blinked.

"These are savages?" he found himself asking.

Someone sat down beside him and he saw that it

was Philippe. "I recognized you across the circle," Philippe said. "I might have known that you'd find your way to the camps."

Peter was still staring at the Indians with such a puzzled look that Philippe smiled. "You are surprised that all these people of the forest are not the half-wild animals Europeans think they are?" he asked. "I was too, before I lived among them. I learned that an Indian will die for a friend he loves. Yet he can be cruel and savage in revenge if he has been wronged."

"I can see I'd rather have an Indian for a friend than an enemy," Peter said.

Suddenly loud cries rose from a group of Indians. A chief with feathered headdress raised a hatchet high as he sprang to face the council.

"From the land of the plains we brought no furs to trade. Therefore we have no blankets to take to our wigwams. We have no French muskets or gunpowder. Our children and our women cry for food. We return to them with empty hands.

"Where are the gifts promised us? We gave our braves in battle. We hunt no more. We fight for the white man and he gives us broken promises for our reward."

Peter looked at Philippe as cries rose from other

Indians in the council ring. "He is right! We were promised gifts! The gifts came but we were forced to pay for them with our furs!"

Montcalm's voice rose above the others. "I have heard of your wrongs, my brothers. But do not let this misunderstanding turn you from fighting with your true brothers for your homeland."

"Misunderstanding!" Philippe muttered.

The Indians broke into such a clamor that Philippe had to lean close to Peter to make himself heard. "The general can do nothing with La Friponne, and he knows it—but he is desperate. He must have the Indians' help."

He motioned Peter and Bomazeen to follow him. The two boys left the crowd of angry Indians with Philippe.

When they reached the river where they could talk without being overheard Philippe said, "Now you know how La Friponne cheated the Indians of their furs. Bigot's bateaux brought the chests of blankets, food, and ammunition to the Indians as they were supposed to do. But Cadet would not unload the chests until the Indians paid again with their furs. The Indians needed the supplies so much that they did as Cadet told them."

Peter felt his face flush with anger. "This is surely the proof General Montcalm needs against La Friponne," he said.

"General Montcalm's records may bring the thieves of La Friponne to justice in the French courts someday," Philippe said, "but not in time to save the Indian furs—or their faith in white men's promises."

The cries from the Indian council grew louder. Peter saw that half the Indians were on their feet. It looked as if they were preparing to leave. What if they failed General Montcalm now, when the English fleet was coming?

"What can we do?" he asked.

"We will take the furs and return them to the Indians," Philippe said quietly. "Do you know where the furs are stored in the great warehouse?"

Peter felt a thumping as loud as a drum in his chest. "Yes," he said.

"I will go with you," Bomazeen said. "The furs are ours."

"It will have to be tonight," Philippe said. "The Hollandais will be anxious to get back to Albany with such a prize load of furs—but Cadet won't dare to load their bateaux until Quebec is asleep.

"We must load the furs from the warehouse before Cadet does," Philippe continued. "I have two bateaux here and coureurs de bois to pole them. We must hurry."

Peter looked down at his Indian clothing.

"Keep them," Bomazeen said. "There is no time to get your wet clothes."

Peter stepped into one of Philippe's bateaux. Bomazeen was right. He must think only of getting the furs from the warehouse without being caught.

VII. Discovery

The sun was setting when the coureurs de bois brought the two bateaux alongside the wharf of the Lower Town. Peter looked at the giant warehouses, closed and shuttered, forbiddingly dark against the gray evening. He shivered. Even though the furs belonged rightfully to the Indians, his palms felt cold and wet at the thought of stealing them from the warehouse.

Philippe spoke to him in a low voice. "Bomazeen will keep watch near our bateaux. You must enter the storehouse through a window—then reach the loading doors. Wait until you hear me call that all is clear outside before you lift the bar and open the door."

Peter nodded and pointed to one of the middle sections. "The furs are stored there," he said.

"Open only wide enough for a man to come through with a pack of furs," Philippe said. "We want no gaping door if a guard passes."

"*Oui*," Peter said, his heart thumping. He made himself cross the wharf slowly, as if he were taking an evening stroll. Beside the warehouse, he flattened himself in the shadows. He heard no sound except the lapping of the water against the pilings.

He followed along the wall of the warehouse until he came to a pile of lumber which he knew to be there. It smelled as fragrant as the pines of the forest as he climbed it. From the top of the pile he was able to reach a small high window used for ventilating the building.

He opened the shutters, climbed through, and dropped down into the pitch-blackness of the room. For seconds he crouched there listening. Could anyone have heard his fall? The darkness was as quiet as a tomb. Peter groped his way along a rough wall until he felt a wooden bar across a door. He pulled it and went into the storehouse beyond.

Even in the dark he could feel the vast space about him and smell the musky odor of the furs. He stumbled over a stack of fur packs, caught himself, then followed along the wall until he reached the loading doors. Here he waited. It seemed a long time until he heard Philippe's whisper. "Peter, open up."

He lifted the bars and felt his heart jump at the loud creak when he pushed the door to let Philippe slip inside. Five coureurs de bois followed at once and were lost in the blackness beside Peter.

"This way," Peter whispered.

The men worked fast, and Peter and Bomazeen helped. But it was several hours before the two large bateaux were loaded with furs.

"La Friponne took three bateaux of furs from the Indians," Philippe said when they were finished. "We have stacked our two bateaux as high as we can; even so, we must leave the cheats more furs than they deserve."

"Hurry," one of the coureurs de bois growled, "or you will also leave your skin."

Philippe laughed as the poling oars plopped into the water. "You must remain," he said to Peter, "to bolt the loading doors again from the inside so no one will discover the loss until we've got away. We need an hour's start to get these back to the Indian camps without trouble."

"I will bar the door and go as I came—through the window," Peter whispered.

"Return to work in the morning as usual," Philippe said as the bateaux moved away. "That way they will never suspect you."

Inside the warehouse, Peter drew the great door tight and shot the heavy bar. He knew his way across this vast room now, even in the blackness. He was congratulating himself upon how perfectly Philippe's plan had worked when he came to the window and realized that it was too high for him to reach, even with the tips of his fingers. His heart beat suffocatingly. Outside he had had a pile of lumber for a ladder. What could he use here?

He remembered the packs of furs and began to drag them from the storehouse into the smaller room. When he had piled six bundles, he tried to climb them, but they rolled and sent him tumbling. He sat up, his ears ringing from the crack of his head against the floor.

These bundles did not pile well. He would have to build them like stairs. He carried more furs and laid four packs flat on the floor under the window, placed three on top of these, wedging them into the crevices between packs, then two, then one.

With his lifted arm he measured the height of the pile. Not quite high enough. He needed another pack. Just as he reached the storeroom door he heard men's voices, low, guarded.

One of the men lighted a lantern. Peter's knees grew weak. He could not move when he saw at the far end, just inside the loading doors, the two Hollandais traders with Cadet. The former butcher's big moon face stood out in the light of the lantern he lifted to show the way. In the wavering shadows his heavy shoulders seemed half as wide as the door.

Peter drew back quickly and his hand struck the wall.

"What was that?" one of the Hollandais asked.

The men paused and Peter thought they would hear his terrified breathing. In a moment they would discover that many of the furs were gone.

"You tremble at a rat," Cadet said with his ugly laugh.

The men advanced again. Peter saw the Hollandais rubbing their hands together as they had when they looked upon the rich furs at the card table. Then Cadet bellowed like an angry animal. "Thieves! Our furs have been stolen!"

Peter was too panic-stricken to move. He saw the lantern raised high and the eyes of the men search the room. He longed to run, but he knew he must not budge. He could not get past the men to the loading door, and the window behind him was too long a reach.

He leaned against the rough walls squeezing himself into the corner behind the door, pushing into it until his neck and back ached from strain.

"The door to the next room is open!" he heard Cadet shout. There was the sound of running feet and approaching light moved across the floor. He knew he had no choice now. He must get through the window or be caught.

He ran across the room and reached the top of the packs of fur. Straining sideways, he clasped one hand over the sill. His cheek scraped against the wall as he stretched to reach it with his other hand. His fingers caught and clung, but he could not pull himself over the sill of the open window.

He heard the men almost at the door of the room. He felt that he would faint from fright and fall back into their hands. *"Bon Dieu,"* he prayed.

He closed his eyes and concentrated on saving his life. I must find the strength. I *must!* He drew deep long breaths to fill his lungs with the air he needed for his effort. His arms shook as he drew himself up and forced the weight of his body upon them. Miraculously he found himself clambering up the wall, digging into the roughness with his moccasins. He pulled himself onto the sill.

He felt the hands of one of the men slide off his legging as he climbed through the small window onto the lumber.

"An Indian!" Cadet shouted. "We can't follow him. The window's too small. Cut him off at the wharf."

Peter leaped from the lumber. He must run faster than the men inside. He passed the loading doors and heard the men lift the bar and shout to the voyageurs waiting in the Hollandais' bateaux. He ran as he had never run before, striking across the beach toward the buildings of the Lower Town which he could see in the gray night. The sound of running feet pursued him. He could not go to his loft at the Fleur de Lys. His Indian clothes would betray him if Cadet followed him there.

He cut through back yards and between buildings until he reached Mountain Hill. Halfway up the steep rough path he felt his strength almost gone, but he must not stop. By the time he reached the Upper

Town, his chest pained so sharply that he longed to fall down full length upon his face in one of the terrace gardens and hide in the dark. He felt that he couldn't run a step farther even if he was discovered.

Then he heard heavy feet on the path behind him. The men were grunting with strain, but they were determined. Peter ran on.

As he passed dark houses, he noticed that he had turned down the street where the Bonheurs lived. He and Philippe had gone into the third house. He reached it and stopped.

He stood in the shadow of the roses which grew over the door. I cannot run any farther, he thought. I cannot.

"I saw him go this way," he heard a voice say. It was Cadet's.

Almost without knowing what he did, Peter reached out and lifted the latch on the door of Marie's house. It opened. He went inside, closed the door, and stood with his back to it.

He tried to control his gasps for breath. He would not awaken Marie and the old man, only wait here until the men had gone by. Then he would leave.

Seconds later he was startled to see Marie come through a door with a candle in her hand. Her dark curls hung loose over the red cape which covered her long nightgown. She cried out and almost dropped her light.

"It is I," Peter said hurriedly. "Philippe's friend."

She drew nearer. "I thought you were an Indian."

Before he could say another word, there was a knock on the door. Peter drew back into the shadows of a corner.

"*Pardon, Mademoiselle Bonheur*," Cadet said as Marie opened the door a crack. "We saw your light and thought you might have been disturbed by the thieving Indian we are searching for."

Peter knew that Cadet had as many different tones of speech as he had customers. This was the voice he used to respected families of the town who were not to be offended.

Peter held his breath. Would Marie give him away? Was she still angry with him for working for La Friponne?

"I have seen no Indian," Marie said. "I am often up at night with my *grandpère*."

She closed the door.

Peter stood in front of the girl and ran his hand through his rusty black hair. "*Merci beaucoup*," he said.

"So—La Friponne has turned on you too," she said coldly, "and in such a short time."

"You do not understand," he said. He poured out to her the story of the night and the rescue of the Indian furs.

"You cannot go into the street again," she said when he had finished. "You shall sleep here tonight. In the morning my *grandpère* will know what to do."

When she had shown him the spare room and closed the door Peter took off his Indian clothing and crawled between linen sheets. The sheets were smooth and strong, made to last for a hundred years. As Peter pulled the hemstitched fold under his chin, the fragrance of lavender caused him to close his eyes in sudden overpowering remembrance of his mother.

He had been so young that he had almost forgotten the great carved chest where his mother kept sheets as fine as these—dozens of sheets. Three or four times a year a washerwoman had come to his home and there was a great laundering of the linens, with soft water and soap, and steam as thick as fog in the stone kitchen. On these days his father wrote in the garden and his mother did not have the time to sing to him as she usually did.

Peter felt as if he were going to cry and he covered

his face with his arms. He must think of the forest, the fragrance of the pines and spruces, the song of the wind in the boughs, the deep peace. The pleasant feeling of home had come to him in the wilderness. He thought hard of these things to overcome his nostalgia and go to sleep.

When he awakened, the sun was shining in his window and he could smell food cooking. He dressed and went into the living room. Grandpère Bonheur sat in his chair by the fireplace. Marie came from the kitchen. They smiled and wished him good morning. Marie showed him where he could wash. When he returned she had placed steaming bowls of soup on the table.

When they were seated the old man clasped his hands and they bowed their heads. Peter recognized the old Latin grace which the Abbé had taught him and recited it with them, asking the blessing of God upon the table and all those who sat around it. *"Benedic, Domine, nos et haec tua dona."*

With the delicious soup there were little oval loaves of wheaten cakes in a basket of silver filigree, cups of hot rich chocolate, hard-boiled eggs, and a bowl of ripe strawberries with their green stems and green frilled caps left on them.

"They are almost too pretty to eat," Peter said finally, choosing a deep red berry shaped like a heart.

"I notice you did not think the same of the eggs," the old man said and chuckled.

Peter looked down at the mound of eggshells in his empty bowl. It looked as if he had eaten a half-dozen, although he was sure it had been only four.

"Never mind," Marie said. "Grandpère loves to see you eat. He says that the mark of a true Frenchman is his appreciation of good food. The strawberries are a gift from the Recollects. The friars have a little garden under glass where they can hurry the ripening of strawberries."

"Father Breyer was pleased because their strawberries were earlier than the Jesuits'." Grandpère Bonheur laughed. "The Recollects like to be ahead in something—you see, the Jesuits go everywhere and bring back flowers from many places, so their gardens are showplaces."

"I must see their gardens," Peter said. "In France I often helped the Abbé with his flowers."

The front door of the house opened and a young man came into the living room.

"Good morning, Major," Grandpère Bonheur said, motioning him to a chair at the table, while Marie poured another cup of chocolate.

"This is the boy Marie told you about earlier this morning." The old man turned to Peter. "This is my grand-nephew, Major Joannes."

"Good morning, sir," Peter said.

"My cousin is the town major of Quebec," Marie said proudly. "We asked him to help find you another place to work. You can't return to La Friponne now."

"Are you commander of the hornworks and the other ramparts that guard the city?" Peter asked the major.

"I command the volunteer militia of the city," Major Joannes answered. "Ramezay commands Quebec's military forces which guard the city walls, and Captain Fiedmont commands the artillery."

"Then the town suffers from divided command," Peter said, "as General Montcalm does in the army —with Governor Vaudreuil."

By the sudden silence, he knew he had said the wrong thing. He remembered that Philippe had told him that Governor Vaudreuil was a native-born Canadian and that the habitants were loyal to him.

The old man was the first to speak. "Governor Vaudreuil loves this town and would do anything to save it," he said, "but he does not have Montcalm's military experience, and he is so jealous of the general that it clouds his judgment at times."

"I do not care who commands," Major Joannes said in such a passionate voice that Peter was stirred, "as long as the white flag of France continues to fly above these ramparts. I will starve; I will die if I must. For this rock and this land belong to France. They must remain French."

"May *le bon Dieu* please," the old man said brokenly. Tears streamed down his cheeks. Marie sat as if in prayer.

Peter's hands gripped the seat of the chair on which he sat. A lump rose in his throat. He was surprised by the strange emotion sweeping through him. He had come to this new world to win his fortune in furs, but the strange land had taken a hold upon him. Suddenly this rock, this home, and these people seemed as dear to him as the Abbé's garden, as his home in France where his father was born and had died. Quebec *must* be saved from the English!

Peter turned to the old man. "Don't Bigot and Cadet love France? Don't they care if we lose?"

"*Oui*, Bigot, at least, cares," the old man said. "That is the strange part of it. Bigot is a member of a fine family of France, but he was too long in the court of the selfish king. Profit and pleasure blind him to what he owes his country. Bigot believes that Quebec is too strong to be taken, and war is an opportunity to make himself rich."

Peter was learning fast that war was a complicated business. Jealousy of command and profiteering could lose a war, even when a country was defended by gallant officers and brave soldiers.

"Quebec is not safe," Major Joannes said. "We begged Bigot for carts and bateaux to bring stone to strengthen the walls of the town and our hornworks, and to bring more food from Three Rivers and Montreal. Bigot says he has no carts or bateaux to spare, yet he uses the king's bateaux to trade far and wide and fill his own pockets."

"There are always men who look to their own profit," Grandpère Bonheur said, "and expect others to save their country."

Peter thought fast. What was *he* doing to help Quebec? Philippe had said that General Montcalm had kept records that would prove Bigot's guilt, and the affair of the Indian gifts would add to the evidence against the man. Peter was no longer needed at La Friponne.

Major Joannes rose from the table. "I will do what I can to find you work, boy," he said.

"*Merci*, but do not trouble yourself," Peter answered. "I have decided to join General Montcalm's army camps before the town."

"You are too young to fight," Marie protested.

"There must be something I can do when the English come," Peter insisted.

Grandpère Bonheur smiled. "*Ma chérie*," he said to Marie, "have you not learned—when a Frenchman makes up his mind to do something, he sees every reason to do it, and none against it?"

VIII. Drummer Boy for Montcalm

Shortly after noon Peter walked through Upper Quebec to the Palace Gate, in the back wall of the town. He carried a letter from Major Joannes to Colonel Bougainville, third in command at Montcalm's headquarters.

Grandpère Bonheur had told Peter that Montcalm had ordered a bridge of boats built across the St. Charles River to reach the army camp. Over these anchored boats soldiers could march quickly if they were needed in Quebec. From the Palace Gate, Peter saw the irregular outlines of the bridge.

He passed a few farmhouses and trees outside the walls, cut across a meadow dotted with white daisies, shiny yellow buttercups, and red Indian paintbrush. When he came upon the bridge he stood above the water and watched the feverish activity farther down, where the St. Charles River emptied into the St. Lawrence. A boom of logs lay in the water across the mouth of the St. Charles. Men were pounding stakes, shoving boulders, and anchoring the logs with chains so that enemy ships could not enter the St. Charles.

Peter wished that the stretch of the St. Lawrence River just above Quebec could be protected in this way. But the mighty St. Lawrence was a mile wide, its current too deep and swift for a log boom—even if the army had not needed it open to transport additional supplies from Montreal and Three Rivers.

When he had crossed the St. Charles River, Peter found himself in the right flank of the French camps. He could see army tents covering the flats all along the shore. Philippe had told him that the camps extended to the Montmorency River, which emptied into the St. Lawrence six miles below. The entire six miles of harbor shore bristled with earthworks, cannon, and soldiers.

Peter came upon some soldiers seated before a tent, cleaning their muskets. He asked for Colonel Bougainville. The men stopped singing and watched him curiously.

"Colonel Bougainville commands this right flank,"

a bearded soldier answered, "but he has gone to the center camp to confer with our general, the Marquis de Montcalm."

The bearded soldier looked at Peter's doeskin shirt and leggings. "Our general has only now returned from the Indian council," he said. "Did you come with him?"

Peter flushed, thinking how these soldiers would shout and laugh if they knew how he came to be wearing Indian clothes.

"No," he said, "I must see Colonel Bougainville."

"It is a walk," the bearded one said. "When you reach center camp you'll see a stone house among many tents in the flax fields. The house is the manor of Seigneur de Salaberry, but it was given over to General Montcalm for headquarters."

Peter approached the stone house and waited nearby. He could not bring himself to knock upon the door of the Marquis de Montcalm, general of the army of France.

The sun beat upon his bare head and the Beauport flats steamed with unusual heat for a day so early in June. It seemed a long time before Peter saw a well-fed young officer leave the house and mount a horse tied to a hitching post. Peter ran and called to him.

"*Pardon,* sir, can you be Colonel Bougainville?"

When the man nodded, Peter handed him Major Joannes's letter.

Colonel Bougainville frowned as he shook open the paper, but his face changed as he read it. He looked up and smiled. "I have just heard of the affair of the furs," he said. "They arrived at the council this morning in time to turn the tide with the Indians. I have never seen General Montcalm more pleased with a coup."

Though Peter couldn't help feeling happy and proud, he said, "Philippe d'Argons deserves the credit for the furs. But I do hope for a place in the army."

Colonel Bougainville looked thoughtful. "We need all the help we can get," he said, "yet you are too young to fight." His face brightened. "Can you play a drum? General Montcalm's own command lost a drummer boy in our last battle. No boy we have tried since seems able to learn the language of the drums but confuses the soldiers by sounding the wrong orders."

Peter felt his own heart beating like a drum. "I can learn," he said. "I'll study—and never beat a wrong order. You shall see."

For two weeks Peter studied and imitated the drum major, a tall older boy whose skill with the sticks upon a drumhead awed Peter. He was issued a drum and a blue uniform. He practiced at the edge of the parade ground, where scores of drummers led their squads in drill.

Peter's wrists ached and the drum strap cut into his shoulder as he drummed and marched daily across the flats and down the river embankment. About! Turn! He signaled with the correct beat just as if he had a troop behind him.

He memorized the language of the drums. There was reveille to wake the men from their beds in the morning. A mess call brought them running from all corners for food. Another roll, the tattoo, ordered them to turn in at night.

On parade and in battle the commands of the officers must be relayed to the soldiers, each with its own special beat.

There were tucks or rolls or ruffles which meant left, right, advance, retreat. Others called to the men to raise their rifles, to thrust at arms' length, to fire. There was the stirring marching-to-battle beat. And there was drum language for the ears of other troops if his squad was in danger, the summons for help—
au secours!

When, at last, Peter was placed at the head of his own squad he stood on the parade ground, trying to keep his hands from trembling. He knew if he made a mistake he could throw his men out of step or even send them in the wrong direction. As he waited for the officer's shout, *"En avant!*—Forward march!"— sweat broke out on his upper lip. He dared not lift his arm to wipe it away. He must be ready. The command came. Behind him he heard fifty pairs of boots come down to the thump of his drum.

Then excitement drove away his anxiety. The blue uniform, the gold braid crisscrossed down the sides of the drum, the feel of the sticks, satin-smooth in his fingers, the boom and rhythm, set his blood racing. When he rolled the dismissal order and his own men threw their hats in the air and shouted, *"Vive le petit tambour!*—Hurrah for the little drummer!"—he was proud enough to burst the gold buttons from his jacket.

Peter's squad lived in tents close to the stone headquarters of General Montcalm. Each day Peter saw the general ride off on his favorite dark bay horse to direct preparations in all parts of the camp. Sometimes Montcalm was in the saddle fifteen to eighteen hours before returning, exhausted, to the stone house.

Wherever General Montcalm went the soldiers cheered him and sang. In spite of the tension of waiting for the arrival of the English fleet and the attack, the men were gay. Peter liked to sing with them around a bonfire at night. It seemed to give them courage to end each evening with the victory song they had made up after defeating the English at Lake George.

> *Je chante des François,*
> *La valeur et la gloire,*
> *Qui toujours sur l'Anglois*
> *Remportent la victoire!*
>
> I sing of the men of France,
> So brave and so glorious,
> Who over the English foe
> Are ever victorious!

Around the campfires the soldiers talked too, and Peter listened. Through some grapevine of their own, they seemed to know all that went on in the camps to the right and left as well as in Montcalm's own headquarters camp in the center. Soldiers going back and forth to Quebec, to visit the taverns, to play cards and dance and call on people in their homes, brought back the news from the town.

They knew toward the end of June when scouts raced to Quebec, from the cliffs of Gaspé, to say that ships had been sighted at sea. The people of Quebec hoped that these would prove to be ships sent from France to engage the English fleet before it reached the town.

"But," said the soldier who had brought the news, "Montcalm has little doubt that they are the English —and the battle is upon us."

The soldiers knew when Chevalier François de Lévis, with his fine troops from Montreal, arrived to reinforce the camps.

"Our general pressed Lévis against him as if he were welcoming a long-lost brother," one soldier said. "Montcalm really loves Lévis."

"In spite of the fact that Lévis gets along well with Governor Vaudreuil," another said and grinned.

"The chevalier has been placed in command of the left flank along the River Montmorency," the first soldier said. "His Montreal troops, with Canadians and Indians, will defend the river and that end of the harbor shore."

That night as Peter lay on his bed of straw in his tent, he could feel his heart beating fast with excitement. Ships had been sighted at last. The time of waiting was almost over.

IX. Ships and Fire Rafts

Peter was awakened by a shout. He scrambled to pull back the flap of his tent. In the gray dawn a courier ran through the rows of tents toward the stone headquarters of General Montcalm.

"Ships!" he shouted. "Ships coming up the channel!"

Before Peter could button his uniform, he heard officers shouting for reveille. He caught up his drum and stumbled out of the tent. Beating the call with all his strength, he brought soldiers tumbling from their tents, dressing as they ran.

Officers shouted. Drums rolled. Soon Peter's own troop formed behind him. The officer cried *"En avant!"* Peter drummed the march to the shore.

He waited with hundreds of soldiers drawn up along the banks of the St. Lawrence behind the defense of earthworks. When the first excitement died down and no sails appeared, the soldiers shifted about restlessly and grumbled. Was this someone's nightmare? they inquired loudly. Were they routed from their beds, marched on empty stomachs, only to stand and gaze on the quiet harbor they saw every day?

"Look," Peter shouted, "ships' canvas—there, with the sun on them!"

The lines of soldiers turned as one body and strained their eyes to watch the approaching fleet. Then a great shout went up from hundreds of throats. The ships flew the white flag of France!

An old soldier pounded Peter on the back. Tears streamed down his cheeks. "Our king *did* send a fleet to overcome the English! These are French ships arriving! We are saved!"

Peter's heart beat hard. It was true. The first ship had reached the far end of the dangerous channel where river pilots must be taken aboard. A French flag climbed its masthead and signaled the pilots to come from the wharf and bring the ship safely into the harbor.

Peter heard the French pilots singing joyfully as they launched their canoes and paddled to meet the fleet. When they drew within a few yards of the ships their songs stopped abruptly. The first pilots struggled to turn their canoes and shouted warnings to the pilots behind.

The guns of the ships boomed and churned water about the canoes. The French pilots had been tricked! Several jumped overboard and tried to swim the swift current to escape. Others were helpless while their canoes were captured by English sailors with long grappling irons. In minutes the pilots were pulled on board and made prisoners.

Then, on all the ships together, the white flags of France fluttered down. The Red Cross of St. George ran to the top of each ship's mast.

For a long moment not a sound came from the stupefied soldiers watching from the shore. Then a soldier beside Peter spoke in a strangled voice. "They'll force our own pilots to bring the English fleet safely through the channel."

Peter's hands closed tightly on his drumsticks. These English were not only clever but treacherous.

Before the day was done their fleet would be anchored in the harbor below Quebec! He saw dozens
of English ships lined on the blue waters: ships-of-
the-line, frigates, sloops-of-war, and more great
troop transports than he could count.

A peculiar feeling moved through Peter. It was
not so much fear as the feeling of dreaming with his
eyes open. He had expected the English, had drilled
with the troops to be prepared to meet them. Yet
the enemy had not seemed real until now.

In a few hours I may be in battle, he thought.

But Montcalm was too wise to be coaxed from
behind his strong fortifications. All day Peter saw
the general in conference after conference with his
officers about a round table inside the open door of
the stone house. He heard an officer pleading excitedly to attack.

"The English are landing on the Isle d'Orléans,"
the officer said. "Governor Vaudreuil sent me to remind you that if the English entrench themselves on
the island they will have a perfect base from which
to harry and destroy us."

Montcalm's voice rose in sarcastic fury. "Remind
Governor Vaudreuil that it is *he* who sent our few

French ships up the Saint Lawrence toward Montreal, for their safety. Does the governor expect my soldiers to swim and attack the English fleet?

"No. *We* hold Quebec. If the English Wolfe wants the town, let him take it from us," Montcalm declared.

The next day was cloudy and cold and another plan was on everyone's lips. Fire rafts were to be sent against the English ships that night, while clouds made the river black.

"We'll burn every English ship right in the harbor," a young soldier said jubilantly.

Some of the men who sat on the ground and ate their thin soup and hard biscuit looked doubtful.

"Fire rafts are a crazy idea," an older soldier said. "General Montcalm puts no faith in them. They are the governor's pet scheme."

"I hear the fire rafts cost a million francs," another soldier said. "I wish they'd spend as much on decent food for us."

"You should be a hen in the barnyard of Bigot," a fourth man growled. "I hear there is plenty of grain for the intendant's fowls—though none for our bread."

When it was very dark Peter joined a group of

whispering soldiers. "It must be almost time. Let's go."

They climbed a rise of the battlements below Beauport Church, which stood in the camp. From here they could overlook the channel where the rafts must pass. From the shuffle of feet, Peter knew that many soldiers were arriving. In the black night their hoarse whispers reached him as from a spirit world.

"It will take steady nerves to guide those fire rafts through the channel with no lights," one voice said. "And our sailors on the rafts must wait until they are among the English ships before they can set the rafts afire. Then powder and shot and flames will fly in every direction. Our men have to escape their own explosions as well as the English guns."

"Tonight I'm glad I'm not in the navy," another voice declared.

The men grew suddenly quiet. Peter felt the hair on the back of his neck prickle. Yes, there was the soft sound of oars in the water. The fire rafts must be gliding through the dark water toward the English fleet anchored in the river.

"*Mon Dieu*, do not let the English hear," Peter prayed.

Suddenly, without sound, tongues of fire leaped above the blackness of the river. Flames burst from a dozen places in quick succession. Great clouds of smoke belched into the sky, pierced by streaks of fire like lightning.

Peter broke into a sweat. His voice shook as he shouted, "We did it! We've set the English ships on fire!"

"Can't you see?" a soldier answered, and he was weeping. "Someone gave the order too soon. The torch was set to our fire rafts before they reached the English."

Explosion after explosion shattered the air as flames swept through the fireworks, bombs, and grenades on the rafts. Grapeshot rattled so near that Peter ducked, trembling at the roar of fire and the hiss of burning objects striking the water. The whole sky was lighted as if it were day.

In the red glare Peter saw the city of Quebec perched upon Cape Diamond. The tents of his own camp lay exposed upon the riverbank. In the river English sailors swarmed the decks of their ships. They launched small boats and came to meet the fire rafts. With grappling irons they caught the blazing rafts and towed them away from the fleet.

Other rafts ran ashore, unmanned now, since the French sailors had leaped into the water.

Only one raft reached the English ships. Peter saw that a dozen gallant men had remained with it until they were under the hull of a frigate. Then they leaped into the water among the hissing debris.

Neither Peter nor the soldiers standing with him on the battlement could speak as they watched the stranded fire rafts burn themselves out at the edge of the water. At last hearty English voices were heard from the river. "All's well. All's well here!"

For a long time after Peter returned to camp he lay in his tent and could not sleep. A lump in his throat bothered him. He took a drink from his canteen, but it did not help. He blinked rapidly. The smoke from the wasted fire rafts must be smarting his eyes.

He turned on his blanket. *C'est fini*—that's the end of that, he said to himself. Tomorrow our General Montcalm will think of a better plan.

X. Fleeing Quebec

As the days and weeks passed, General Montcalm stuck to his original plan, to hold the camps and the town. Let the English attack if they dared.

In addition to the English fleet in the St. Lawrence, English forces occupied the Isle d'Orléans and the south shore of the river, as well as the left bank of the Montmorency River. When the English Wolfe began building parapets on Point Lévis, directly opposite Quebec, General Montcalm ordered the French batteries guarding the narrows of the St. Lawrence to raise their sights and fire on Point Lévis. But the French cannon were too small and their balls fell harmlessly into the river.

Helplessly the French watched while the English built their entrenchments on Point Lévis and trained their cannon upon the town. When the English guns began to fire, smoke rose above the walls of Quebec. Peter saw that Wolfe's cannon were heavy enough to place shells across the river though the French cannon were not.

Smoke from the burning town lay like fog over the camps. Couriers came daily to Montcalm to tell him of the helpless people and the burning homes. Montcalm sent troops of soldiers into the town to fight the fires.

Peter longed to know whether Philippe and Marie and Grandpère Bonheur were safe, but he had no way of finding out and would not be given leave to go into the town until he had been in camp a month.

Each day Peter heard the soldiers complain more loudly against the inaction of the army. "We are meat in the sandwich, between the English across the Montmorency and the English burning the town," they said.

At last Montcalm must have felt that they needed encouragement. He ordered his officers to have the drummers call the men of center camp together before his headquarters, where he could talk to them as he often did before a battle.

When Montcalm came from the stone house the assembled soldiers grew as quiet as small boys caught whispering in school. The general mounted his bay horse so all could see him and called over the throng in his rapid, fiery voice.

"I have sent a message to General Wolfe, under flag of truce, asking him to spare the town. I have told him that he might demolish Quebec, but that you, my brave men, would never let him inside its walls."

"*Vive! Vive notre général!*—Hurrah for our general!" the men shouted. They cheered until Montcalm lifted his hand. Peter saw the lace of his cuff fall back against his white and gold uniform.

"Wolfe replied that he will have the town if he has to stay here until November," Montcalm said.

A buzz of hatred ran through the men like fire through forest treetops. Peter felt his own cheeks burn.

"Before November his ships will be frozen in the river!" a soldier cried. "We will cross on the ice and pull his men from their decks by the ear—one by one. Tell that to the English Wolfe!"

Montcalm motioned again for silence.

"We are short of supplies, both food and ammunition. We have no ships to match the English on water. We cannot attack. But you are right about winter's hazards. The English fleet cannot remain here safely past the middle of September. We must hold Quebec until the English are forced to leave.

"We are saved if we remain alert both day and

night. Our camps are strong and can repulse any attack here. Our town batteries must prevent any English ship from going up the Saint Lawrence River above Quebec. The English armies on the south shore are helpless to reach the north shore without ships above the town. That is our plan—to repulse and wait for winter."

"*Vive! Vive notre général!*" the soldiers shouted again. They were once more confident when they understood Montcalm's plan.

As the men moved off, Peter stood by the hitching rail. The flank of Montcalm's horse brushed his arm, but he could not speak to the great man. Then he heard Montcalm's voice.

"You must be the boy of the furs—of whom Colonel Bougainville told me," Montcalm said.

Peter looked up and could only nod.

"I'm told that you too came from the South of France," Montcalm said. "Tell me—did you live near my home, the Château de Candiac?"

"No, sir," Peter managed to say.

Such tenderness and homesickness came into the general's eyes that Peter felt his own eyes smart. "I hoped you might have something to tell me of home," Montcalm said. Then, as if he had forgotten Peter: "Candiac, Candiac, will I ever see your sunny fields again, my grapes and my olive trees—my dear wife—my children?"

The general wheeled his bay horse abruptly and rode away.

That evening Peter had just finished his supper of wormy biscuit and soup when he saw a man in the uniform of the town militia approaching. After a moment's puzzlement he realized that it was Philippe, and he hurried to meet him.

"Philippe," he cried, "I'm so glad you're safe! And how are Marie and her grandfather?"

"I haven't seen Marie," Philippe said. "We've little time for visiting these days. But Grandpère Bonheur has joined the militia."

Peter stared at Philippe. Grandpère Bonheur was more than eighty years old and crippled with gout. "You must be joking," he said.

"I tried to reason with him," Philippe said, "but he said that he had loved the town—and France— longer than any of us, and that gave him greater reason to defend it."

Peter felt a pain in his chest. He looked at Philippe. "I'm free until bedtime," he said. "Would you like to walk down to the shore and see our new entrenchments?"

As they walked through the dark Philippe said that he had come with Major Joannes, who was conferring with General Montcalm in the stone house.

"We brought bad news," he said. "Last night, under cover of black clouds and with a northeast breeze favoring them, several English ships slipped past our batteries at the mouth of the Saint Lawrence River. We fired upon them, but the ships passed safely and now they are cruising back and forth in the river above the town."

Peter's stomach felt hollow. This was exactly what Montcalm had said must not happen. The shore above the town was undefended. Then he remembered the height of the cliffs there and felt better.

"General Montcalm is sending Colonel Bougainville with some of the best troops to patrol the north shore and keep the ships in sight at all times," Philippe said. "Bomazeen is a courier with him."

"I wish Bomazeen would be sent here with a message," Peter said. "I liked him."

Philippe smiled. "And Bomazeen liked you," he said. "He seemed to think you were brave the night we took the furs."

Peter grinned. "He didn't see me running from Cadet and the Hollandais."

"He heard about it," Philippe said, laughing.

They had come to the entrenchments, which Philippe agreed were strong enough to discourage an English attack on the camps. They scrambled to the top of the earthworks and sat down facing the river. Philippe lighted his pipe, and Peter sat beside him, hugging his knees.

Across the channel on the Isle d'Orléans, Peter could see the glow of English campfires, like great red eyes of monsters glaring at him through the dark. What new destruction was General Wolfe planning there with his soldiers?

"I hate the English Wolfe," Peter said.

"This is an old war between the English and us," Philippe said quietly. "I fought the English at Oswego and Fort Henry, where I was wounded and later discharged from the army. I became a coureur de bois but rejoined the militia when I learned of Quebec's danger."

Peter was proud that Philippe had helped put the English to flight in earlier battles. "We'll win this time too," he said.

Philippe's voice was thoughtful when he finally spoke. "I've heard much about General Wolfe," he said. "He's a clever and brave man, though ruthless."

Rebellion rose in Peter. He had not expected this kind of talk from Philippe about the fiend who burned Quebec and sent a band of rangers over the river at night to burn farmhouses and fields of grain, so that there was no food to be had and everyone was hungry.

"Wolfe really hates war," Philippe went on. "It is said that he studies Latin and French and mathematics at night in his tent—and quotes poetry aloud when he is too exhausted to sleep. He is often ill, and longs to go home and marry the girl who waits for him in England."

"Then why does he fight?" Peter cried. "We'd be happy enough to see him go."

"He is a soldier and his country wants the furs and rich land in the New World. You've seen enough, Peter, to know that this land is worth fighting for."

"But the furs and land belong to us—to France," Peter said.

"And that's why *we* fight," Philippe answered. He knocked out his pipe and stood up. "I must get back," he said. "I have midnight watch at the garrison."

"In a few more days," Peter said, "I'll have leave and see for myself what is happening to Quebec."

When his day of leave came Peter left center camp at daybreak, walked through the right-flank camp, now commanded by Governor Vaudreuil, crossed the bridge of boats over the St. Charles River, climbed the slope of meadow, and entered the back of the town through the Palace Gate. Even at this early hour he met people fleeing from the town. Some walked beside small carts piled high with bedding and clothing; others carried their possessions in their arms.

Although he knew that the town had been under bombardment for days Peter was shocked to see the great holes in the streets and the dark mounds of ashes where homes had been hit and burned.

He passed the intendant's palace, surrounded now by a double row of palisades with field guns mounted on top. Beginning below the palace, battle palisades three feet thick ran along the cliff clear to the Lower Town.

He knew, from talk in the camps, that the Lower Town had been evacuated days ago and Mountain Hill Road was heavily barricaded so no English could climb into the Upper Town if they succeeded in landing on the beach, which seemed impossible.

As Peter turned into the street leading to Marie's

home he was almost afraid to look, for fear it might have been struck. Then he saw roses blooming white and red over the door. As he was about to knock, he heard Marie call to him from the window.

"Peter, you look so grown-up and handsome in that uniform and gold braid—why, I hardly knew you!"

"Better than in Indian clothes?" he asked. They both grinned.

A rumble shook the sky. Marie ran to the door and opened it. "The day's bombardment has begun!" she cried.

Inside, Peter saw that she had piled some of the silver on the polished table. She hurried to the mantel and took the china shepherdess and shepherd and wrapped them in a linen tablecloth.

"Grandpère says I must go outside the west wall to one of the farmhouses where it is safe," she said, "but I cannot bear to leave my mother's precious things here to be destroyed. *Her* mother brought these candlesticks from France. I remember how lovingly my mother polished them."

Peter stood helplessly, not knowing what to say to comfort her. He took up a bundle of her treasures. "I'll help you carry them," he said.

As they crossed the street, hugging their bundles

to them, a bomb struck so close that gravel stung Peter's cheek. He ducked and ran after Marie. They hurried down the slope and reached the far side of the Ursuline convent and pressed their backs against the stone building for protection.

"Peter, let's go into the chapel," Marie said.

He followed her inside. A figure of the Holy Mother had fallen and her arms were shattered on the floor. A portion of the roof had been torn away. Beyond dim shadows Peter saw candlelight flickering on the gold filigree of the altar.

"Nearly all the nuns are helping at the General Hospital," Marie whispered, "but a few remain to tend the altar."

Together they went down the aisle and knelt. When they rose from their prayers Peter saw a bomb crater to the right, close to the railing. The cavity looked almost deep enough and long enough to bury a man.

A heavy rain of shell rattled on the roof. "Hurry! We must get out of the town," he said to Marie.

As they left the chapel it seemed as if the whole town had begun to burn. Great clouds of smoke twisted through the streets. Peter began to choke and he heard Marie coughing. As they ran, shells screamed about their ears; flames reached out from doorways; the earth shook under them from deafening explosions.

People darted through the streets, some carrying bundles. Others carried babies or dragged children by the hand.

Peter and Marie came upon a sea of people crowded against the Palace Gate. A jam of loaded carts, carriages, and wagons barred the opening. No one could get through. Men called instructions. Women shouted. Children cried.

Peter turned to Marie. "We'd better follow the wall until we reach Saint John Gate." She nodded. They groped along the stones through the smoke.

When they were safe outside the walls, in the fresher air of the country, they sat down on the grass to rest.

"I did not dream it was as bad as this," Peter panted. His cheeks were scorched and he longed for a drink of water. "I'm going back to camp—at least the bombs can't reach us there."

"You saw nothing," Marie said. "The cathedral is in ashes. And Major Joannes says that a hundred and sixty-seven buildings burned in Lower Town in one day. Yet many people have to return at night—or sleep on the ground. Besides, we have nothing to eat outside the town. At least inside we are given our ration of four ounces of bread a day."

"So little?" Peter said, shocked. "We are allowed twice that, and still I am always hungry."

"The army has to have food for strength to fight," Marie said.

"Promise you won't go back—for any reason," Peter said.

Marie stood up. "I can stay with friends in that house at the edge of the Plains of Abraham."

Peter helped her carry her bundles to the door-yard, which was crowded with other fleeing peo-ple. He waved good-by and hurried through the meadow toward the bridge of boats.

Suddenly Peter heard a whimper. He stopped and heard the whimper again.

Then he saw a movement in the grass. Some meadow flowers waved as a small body made its way through them. A puppy with a white face and black ears and feet crawled close to him and whimpered again. Its white-tipped tail quivered pleadingly. Peter went down on his knees.

"You're afraid, little fellow," he said, holding the trembling puppy against his check. "In truth, so am I." He has run from Quebec too, Peter thought, and he is too small to care for himself. "How would you like to join the French army?" he asked the puppy.

It licked his face excitedly. Peter grinned and tucked the pup under his arm. He began to sing as he swung along, hoping to cheer himself as well as the little dog. When Peter's voice rose in high notes, the pup joined in with yelps and little drawn-out cries. Peter laughed and began to feel better.

As Peter was crossing the bridge of boats a group of soldiers stopped him. They exclaimed over the pup and sang loudly together for the fun of hearing the little dog try to outcry them.

"What will you take for this one?" a soldier asked, when he could stop laughing.

"Not all the gold you have among you," Peter said. "He is mine. I am going to call him Kébec—after the town."

The men looked toward the flames and smoke.

"We are on our way to reinforce Colonel Bougainville," one of the older soldiers said. "He has full charge above the town from the Plains of Abraham as far up the Saint Lawrence River as the English ships dare to venture."

"I heard that English ships slipped past our batteries," Peter said. "Do you know how many?"

"*Oui*—a fifty-gun warship, a frigate, and five

smaller ships are up the Saint Lawrence. They threaten our line of food and ammunition from Three Rivers and Montreal."

This was worse than Peter had thought.

"Don't look so troubled," said one of the men. "No one seriously believes that enough of these English ships can run past the town's batteries to attack us from above. Yet there has to be a guard to march back and forth and keep watch on them."

A fair-haired boyish soldier groaned. "Much shoe leather will be worn out before winter comes and we're rid of these English."

Slowly Peter walked among the tents of Governor Vaudreuil's camp beside the St. Charles River. He came to the place where the St. Charles emptied into the St. Lawrence and he looked across the water at the four great French batteries guarding the entrance to the St. Lawrence. Farther out in the water, to guard the channel, the French had sunk two of their own ships and mounted guns on them.

He didn't see how English ships had managed to slip past these, but they had. They were cruising the river above the town right now and no matter how closely Colonel Bougainville and his men watched, the English ships were a threat to all supplies and

food shipped down from Three Rivers and Montreal.

"I do not like it," Peter said to Kébec as he started
back to the center camp. "If English ships passed the
town once on a black night, they can do it again."

XI. The Battle of Montmorency

Kébec was an instant success among the soldiers of Peter's troop about the campfire that evening. They laughed as the little dog frisked from one soldier to another, and they fed him thin soup and hard biscuit.

"Not fit for a dog to eat, is it?" a soldier said, rubbing the puppy's ears. "Well, little one, Cadet feeds it to us."

A soldier with a curly black beard fashioned a collar for Kébec. Another cut strips from doeskin and wove a rope: Kébec must be staked beside Peter's tent to keep him safe.

While the men played with the puppy a courier came from the left-flank camp with a tale to tell. That very afternoon, he said, Wolfe had led a force which tried to ford the Montmorency River and surprise the French right flank at the back, but Lévis' troops had been ready for them.

"Our Canadian fighters and Indians lay on their stomachs in the grass and watched the English across the river, making ready for their surprise attack," the visiting courier said jubilantly. "You should have seen the English disorder when eight hundred Indians leaped to their feet with a war whoop—and the Canadians began to shoot."

"*Vive les Indiens! Vive les Canadiens! Vive le Chevalier de Lévis!*" the men cheered.

An older soldier shook his head. "Today will not be the end of it. Wolfe knows he cannot draw us from behind our entrenchments. He must attack."

Early on the last day of July, Peter was awakened by shouts outside his tent. He pulled on his uniform hastily and joined a dozen soldiers nearby who were watching the St. Lawrence River. Peter saw a flotilla of barges bearing regiments of red-coated soldiers come from Point Lévis. Another fleet moved out from Isle d'Orléans. A third group of ships, the decks alive with redcoats, came from down the river.

"They are drawing together!" a soldier cried. "They mean to attack."

"But where?"

Peter could not believe that the English fleet had so many ships. Hundreds of their battleships were lined up in three rows, facing the entire length of French camps on the flats. Artillery fire from the ships began to fall on the French entrenchments along the shore.

Peter heard an officer bawl orders and he ran for his drum. He pulled the sling over his shoulder and drummed the call to assemble.

The troops drew up on the parade ground to await orders. Peter could see Montcalm watching the English ships from his headquarters. At last barges began to move toward the St. Charles River, as if to attack there.

Montcalm ordered his center troops to the right flank to support Governor Vaudreuil. The barges changed course abruptly and moved toward the center section. The troops halted, waited uncertainly.

The hot sun beat down on Peter's head. Sweat trickled along his neck. His hands grew so sticky that the drumstick slipped. While the morning hours passed, the English ships continued to threaten first the center, then the left or right, in an attempt to throw the French troops into confusion.

Suddenly a courier drew up his horse in a cloud of dust before General Montcalm with a message from Lévis. The English were attacking in force along the Montmorency River.

"To the left!" the general ordered. "Reinforce Chevalier de Lévis!"

Almost before he heard his officer's shout Peter's drum began the roll and call. He stepped out briskly, beating time for the long march to the Montmorency. Behind him came the eager tramp of feet. In spite of the stifling heat, which promised another of the frequent thunderstorms, the soldiers were jubilant. They had suffered the English bombing and burning too long. Let the English see what Frenchmen could do! They sang, and Peter sang with them.

> *Je chante des François,*
> *La valeur et la gloire,*
> *Qui toujours sur l'Anglois,*
> *Remportent la victoire!*

In late afternoon the troops came to a halt on the cliffs above the gorge where the Montmorency River fell over two hundred feet into the St. Lawrence. Peter could not take his eyes from the beauty of the plunging white water with its snowy spray and mist of rainbow colors.

Then he saw the boldness of Wolfe's plan. Below, at the foot of the steep clay cliff, were dozens of English ships. They had come in near the falls at high tide. Already two barges, carrying red-coated troops, were stranded on the spongy beach left bare as the tide receded. Across the Montmorency, farther upriver at the ford, thousands of English soldiers were waiting until the tide was low enough so that they could wade across and join their troops from the ships.

Peter heard a cry behind him from thousands of French throats, "*Vive notre général!*"

He turned and saw that General Montcalm had arrived on horseback to confer with Lévis. The chevalier ordered the battalions to draw up ready to repulse the English when they began to climb the steep cliff. An officer shouted an order. It was repeated down the French lines.

"Hold your fire until the English are within range! We are short of powder."

On the waiting English ships below, the red-coated soldiers answered the victory song of the French on the cliff with a taunting parody they sang to the tune of "Lilies of France."

Through the warning crisscross of fire from the French cannon on the cliff, the shouts of the men, and the roar of the waterfall Peter caught snatches of the English words:

Come follow the hero that goes to Quebec . . .
. . . aboard the transports . . . loose every sail,
. . . ye that love fighting shall soon have enough!
Wolfe commands us—we'll give them HOT STUFF!

Suddenly, beside the ford, General Wolfe appeared at the head of his Highland Regiment. Peter knew it had to be Wolfe because of the general's uniform on the frail body with narrow shoulders.

Wolfe was taller than any man about him. His black three-cornered hat was set on red hair which fell in a knot at the back of his neck. His scarlet coat reached to the knees of his thin legs and he wore a black band of mourning around one arm.

He's young and doesn't look like a hero, Peter thought. Can this be the clever Wolfe all Quebec dreads?

A moment later Peter had to admit that Philippe

was right about the courage and daring of the English Wolfe. Wolfe led his Highlanders into the shallow ford and did not even hesitate at the rain of bombs and shot from the French guns and cannon on the cliff.

The tide was low. The battle had begun.

The French batteries of cannon set up a deafening roar as the English dashed forward along the marshy beach and tried to gain the hillside. Peter crouched as the heights beside him blazed with musket shot from the French troops.

A rush of English took over a French redoubt at the foot of the cliff, but as they dashed forward again, struggling to climb the steep sides, Canadian marksmen and Indians rose slightly in the grass and picked them off. Most of the dead and wounded rolled down the cliff and lay upon the beach. Others crumpled on the hillside.

Swarms of English crossed the ford, poured from the boats through the shallow water, tried again to climb the cliff.

Suddenly, above the deafening roar of the artillery and muskets, Peter heard a giant clap of thunder. A zigzag of blinding light cut the horizon and ripped into the tossing water of the St. Lawrence. He looked up from the battle scene to find the sky black with clouds. The promise of storm in the stifling heat was being fulfilled.

As the rain poured down it formed a thin silvery screen between him and the English soldiers who slipped and slid as the hillside turned glistening wet. They no longer looked like soldiers but like troubled men tripping and rolling and falling in the slick clay. Both the English and French powder was instantly wet through. The firing of gun and cannon ceased completely.

The English fell back. Patches of scarlet showed through the mud that covered their coats. With a wave of his arm Wolfe acknowledged the madness of trying to climb the slippery hill again. English trumpets and drums rolled the call for retreat. Wolfe's soldiers began to pick up their dead and wounded and carry them through the ford to their boats.

"*Merci, mon Dieu,*" Peter said fervently with a glance at the sky. The storm was clearing as quickly as it had gathered.

Suddenly his blood froze as shrieks and yells split the air around him. The grass and trees along the heights came alive with half-naked Indians, their bodies painted red and blue. Colored feathers dangled from their scalplocks. They rushed down the

slope toward the helpless wounded English who lay
on the hillside. Peter felt his stomach twist.

He heard a groan to his right and saw a wounded
English soldier a short distance down the slope. The
soldier had half raised himself and was trying to
beat off an Indian with his musket. The Indian
clutched the fair English hair and raised his tomahawk.

Almost without realizing what he was doing Peter
leaped and landed against the back of the Indian,
carrying him onto his knees beyond the wounded
man. The furious Indian turned. Peter threw himself
down the hill as the tomahawk split open the earth
where Peter had been. He jumped up and ran, and
looked back to see several French soldiers race down
the hill and catch the Indian. They held him while
two Englishmen climbed to their wounded comrade
and carried him to the boats.

Peter wiped the perspiration from his forehead
and stopped to catch his breath. What he had said to
Philippe was right—Indians made better friends
than enemies. And maybe there was as much differ-
ence in Indians as in white men. Bomazeen and the
chiefs he had heard in council seemed loyal, brave,
and proud, as well as friendly. But these Indians in
battle were truly savages.

Peter watched the English finish their retreat in good order. They set fire to their stranded barges to keep the French from capturing them. Wolfe and his Highlanders were the last to leave, placing themselves in the rear to protect their troops as they moved across the ford.

"We lost only a handful of men!" a French soldier cried. "The storm saved us."

"Saved *us!*" said another. "Saved the English, you mean. If they had reached the heights we would have killed every one."

It is true, Peter thought. The English lost many men. They will have no taste for attacking our entrenchments again.

Wet and tired, hungry and mud-splattered, the men marched back to camp and found their tents flooded from the storm. Their clothing and bedding were soaked through. Kébec was wet and shivering. Peter carried the puppy to the bonfire the men built. While they dried themselves and their bedding around the flames, they sang far into the night:

.   .   .   .   .

La valeur et la gloire,

.   .   .   .   .

Remportent la victoire!

Holding Kébec against his chest to warm him, Peter sang until his throat grew hoarse. "Victory is good," he told the little dog. "You brought us luck, Kébec."

But at last when he lay in his tent with Kébec beside him, Peter could not sleep. The excitement and action was over. The camp seemed too silent. For the first time that day he could think.

His first battle was over and he hadn't run away, but he'd just as soon never see another. He had nothing to defend himself with under fire but a drum. He could only wait orders and hope he didn't get hit. And he had to admit that his stomach felt sick with sympathy for the dying and wounded, even the hated English.

"Let winter come soon," he prayed, "and drive the English home."

XII. The Siege Drags On

Rejoicing in the French camps turned to gloom as August wore on. Quebec continued to burn. Each dark night, when the wind was northeast, English ships ran past the French batteries guarding the approach to the city. The English fleet above the town grew; there were twenty-two large ships with heavy guns, and many barges which could transport troops from their position on the south shore.

This brought new fears to General Montcalm. At the beginning of the siege Montreal had sent her best troops to defend Quebec. Now, any day, the strong English fleet sailing back and forth in the St. Lawrence River might decide to attack Montreal. Montreal must be reinforced, but who could be spared from Quebec?

At a council of officers held in the stone house Chevalier de Lévis was chosen to return to Montreal with his troops.

Montcalm embraced his friend as Lévis left the headquarters. "I know that you are the man to protect Montreal," the general said, "but I do not know how I shall get along without your counsel, and your calm judgment."

The days grew shorter and the nights colder. Chill rains and wind added to the gloom of the hungry soldiers as August ended.

One night as Peter shivered in his tent Kébec began to bark excitedly. Peter rubbed the pup's ears to quiet him. A head was thrust through the flap of the tent.

"Bomazeen!" Peter cried. "Crawl in; it's warmer here."

The two boys sat on their heels, almost filling the small tent.

"How did you find me?" Peter asked.

Bomazeen laughed. "It was easy. I asked, 'Where sleeps the drummer boy with the dark curly hair and the biggest voice in the army?'"

Peter grinned. "I hope you brought word that Colonel Bougainville is sending us supplies from Three Rivers or Montreal. It is so long since I have eaten a full meal—my stomach complains constantly."

"We know how Bigot and Cadet feed you," Bomazeen said, "although I hear there is plenty to eat for those in the intendant's palace. Colonel Bougainville is with the general now to tell him that he has barges of food hidden against the north bank of the river, but we must wait for a dark night to bring them past the English ships."

"How is it above the town?" Peter asked.

"We march continually—up and back—along the miles of the north shore," Bomazeen answered. "With every tide the English ships float upriver—sometimes as far as Cap-Rouge—and back again on the ebb. We are worn out from following them on foot."

"I know," Peter said. "The rest of their fleet, here before our camp, threatens us night and day, so we can never really sleep. But surely it will be over soon. Everyone thinks they must leave any hour now."

Bomazeen nodded. "Two English deserters joined us yesterday. They said Wolfe's officers of the fleet warned him that it is dangerous to remain in the river any later—and his land officers have told him that it is useless to attack such entrenchments as ours."

"English deserters?" Peter exclaimed in amazement.

"*Oui,*" Bomazeen said. "They want to remain in the New World to live, so they deserted before their ships sail back to England."

Peter leaned forward. "Then the English really mean to leave?" he cried. "*Merci, mon Dieu!*"

"Listen!" the Indian said. "I hear Colonel Bougainville leaving headquarters now. He may need me to carry a message."

The two boys crawled from the tent. They waited when they saw that Montcalm was talking with Bougainville beside his horse.

"You have *carte blanche*—a free hand—above the town," the general was saying. "Remember, the fate of France lies in your hands. But there is little to fear if you take all the precautions we discussed."

Montcalm handed the colonel a letter. "Here are my orders to Governor Vaudreuil. Your courier can take them at once. I have instructed the governor to establish the Regiment of Guyenne on the Plains of Abraham not later than tomorrow.

"The Guyenne and your troops together will be able to hold off any last-minute attempt by the English to land above the town. Meanwhile I will keep my troops in readiness here and come to your aid at a moment's notice if you send for help."

Colonel Bougainville smiled and tapped the orders. "With the fine soldiers of Guyenne on the Plains I can rest easier," he said.

Montcalm's voice sounded more troubled. "Never rest easy until the English are gone, my friend," he said. "For months we have borne hunger and siege as men ought—now that winter is almost here it would be the height of misfortune to be surprised. And I cannot believe that the English Wolfe will crawl off home without one last attack upon us."

On the evening of September twelfth Peter was drawn from his tent by the uproar of heavy bombardment of cannon from the English ships in the river. He saw Montcalm come from the stone house with several officers behind him. Among them were Captains Johnstone and Poulariez, who had been given command of the left flank of the army after Lévis left for Montreal.

Montcalm seemed greatly disturbed. "I fear the English have discovered our convoy of provisions!" he cried.

Captain Johnstone frowned. "It was a great risk

to send a convoy now—when we expect the English to leave any moment."

"We are desperate," Montcalm said. "We must have food and ammunition. We waited for this dark night with a late moon."

Again the guns from the English battleships dropped shot in the French trenches along the shore. In the red flashes of fire Peter saw that the ships were drawn up in battle lines; they shifted toward one side of camp, then another.

"They are trying to confuse us, just as they did before the Battle of Montmorency," Peter said to Kébec, who quivered in his arms and whined at the roar of shot and shell.

One of the officers cried, "This may be the attack we were expecting before the English leave!"

"Or it may be a ruse to draw our attention from the real attack," Captain Johnstone said.

Another said, "These ships could be engaging us so the remainder of the fleet above the town can return past our batteries safely. Their ships upriver must get back here before Wolfe can start for England."

"We can take no chances," Montcalm declared. He shouted the order to assemble.

Officers echoed the order through the camp.
Peter ran for his drum and stood straight, beating the
call. He could hear drums repeating across the camp,
bringing soldiers on the run.

When the troop officers were assembled before
headquarters Montcalm mounted his horse and
spoke to them from the darkness. Only bursts of red
fire crossing between the ships and the French
trenches lighted the shadows of thousands of men
gathered in quietness on the flats.

"My friends, my brave and gallant soldiers—"
Montcalm began.

A queer feeling moved through Peter. He had
never heard his general's voice so emotional. He felt
his own throat tighten.

"I have instructed your officers. Half of you will
man the trenches here; the others will rest with
muskets ready—in reserve for any alarm from another direction."

A shout of *"Vive! Vive le général!"* rose from
thousands of throats.

Peter thought the old cry sounded subdued in the
dark and fog.

Montcalm's horse reared at a sudden thunder of
cannon. He drew rein and it steadied.

"You have stood siege and hunger as men ought," he said. "I can ask no more. Remember, the fate of France lies with you."

Then Peter saw the general ride off in great excitement, as if he would discover for himself the secret of the English plans.

Peter found that his troop was among the reserves. Some of the men returned silently to their tents. Others built bonfires and gathered about them. Dressed ready for battle, with their muskets by their sides, they talked in low tones.

"The tide is right for the English ships to sail toward the sea tonight—and if the wind comes up just a little more . . . ," one began.

"Please, *mon Dieu*," Peter whispered, "please give the English sails the right wind." Kébec whimpered. Peter rubbed the puppy's ears gently. "Never did I think I would pray for wind for English sails," he said, "but if it will help them go home I will pray all night."

Soberly he remembered another night when he had prayed over and over again. He had been very young and he prayed for a day of warm sunshine so he and the Abbé could go walking through the beautiful countryside as they loved to do. He remembered his sobs when it had rained hard all day.

The Abbé had taken him on his knee and stroked his hair, much as Peter was soothing Kébec now.

"The crops need water, Peter," the old man had said. "Perhaps many farmers prayed for rain today. *Le bon Dieu* did not promise always to do what we ask. He promised always to be with us—whether it rains or shines."

XIII. The Plains of Abraham:
September 13, 1759

Peter slept fitfully among the men around the camp-fire and, at dawn, stood and stretched. The fire had burned out. The English ships had ceased bombardment. All seemed quiet, and danger past. He was cold and damp and hungry and wondered if there was anything for breakfast.

He saw Montcalm, who looked as if he had not been to bed all night, standing before the stone house with Captain Johnstone. They were drinking cups of tea together while stableboys saddled fresh horses. Peter saw them lift their heads and listen as he heard a rumble like distant thunder. Soldiers going to their tents after the night's vigil paused and listened too.

Again Peter heard the rumbling sound. A fine misty rain was falling, and it seemed too cold for a thunderstorm. The rumble was repeated. This time he knew it was not thunder but the firing of heavy guns.

The firing sounded too far distant to be that of French batteries in the town. It came from above Quebec, from the direction of the watch at Anse du Foulon. Yet this could not be. There were no heavy guns any place above the town.

Peter joined a group of soldiers gathering silently close to where the general and his companion were standing. He saw Montcalm frown and heard him speak rapidly to Johnstone. "Our worst fears are realized. The English must have discovered our convoy of provisions. Pray God they won't be taken."

Peter breathed more easily. His general believed the firing to come from English ships in the river above the town.

The reports grew louder and heavier. Suddenly the guns of Quebec began to boom. Again Peter saw

Montcalm and Johnstone listen intently. The general became more agitated.

"The town guns are signaling!" he cried. "What can it mean?"

He called for his horse, then sent a courier flying to Governor Vaudreuil, in charge of the flank nearest Quebec, to ask if the governor knew what was happening.

While General Montcalm conferred with several officers who had hurried from their tents to headquarters a Canadian soldier staggered into their midst. He stood before Montcalm, gasping for breath. After several moments he began to babble out a jumble of words, sounding like a madman. One of the officers took his arm to lead him away, but he fell upon his knees.

"The English have seized Anse du Foulon—" he gasped. "Surprised us—in the night. I alone escaped."

The officers exchanged pitying glances. They knew too well the difficulty of climbing the cliffs at the Foulon to believe the man's tale.

"The English are masters on the Heights of Abraham," the man insisted.

"He has gone mad from fear and strain," an officer said.

"Give this sick man food and rest," Montcalm said gently.

"Believe me," the soldier begged. "The English climbed the ravine of Saint Denis Brook."

"Impossible," Montcalm said. "The brook is swollen with rains. There is only a narrow steep path. It is barricaded with fallen trees and trenches."

"A few English climbed the face of the cliff— they must have pulled themselves up by the shrubs, hand over hand," the soldier said. "They tore out the entrenchments on the path. Then the English troops followed from the ships in the river below."

"What of the guard?" Johnstone asked. "Reinforcements were ordered at Foulon."

"No reinforcements came," the soldier said. He shook as if a chill had struck him. "We were sound asleep in our tents—the English surrounded us. I— I—alone—got away." He was mumbling.

"If this were true," Montcalm said, "Bougainville would have attacked the enemy. His courier would have come to us for help."

"How long ago was this?" Johnstone asked.

The Canadian ran a hand over his wet forehead. "Four, maybe five hours. I tried first to reach Colonel Bougainville, but he must have followed the English fleet upriver to Cap-Rouge and failed to return with them. I hid in the woods and heard our watch posts at Samos and Sillery taken by the English—yet Bougainville did not come, so he cannot have realized what has happened."

"The Guyenne Regiment was ordered to the Plains," Montcalm said desperately. "They would have rushed to protect you."

"The Guyenne camped on the Saint Charles last night," the man answered. "Governor Vandreuil sent word that he hadn't enough food or powder to move a regiment. He said he would attend to it tomorrow, when your supplies reached him."

Montcalm's face was a study. Peter could see that he still believed the soldier mad. Everything the Canadian related was too fantastic. In the first place, the cliffs could not be climbed. And even Governor Vaudreuil would not have disobeyed Montcalm's orders to reinforce Anse du Foulon and establish his regiment on the Plains of Abraham without informing the general. Besides, Bougainville always followed the English fleet, keeping it in sight, up the river and back.

But suppose that last night Bougainville had believed the gallant Guyenne Regiment to be on guard in his place and had given his weary men a much-deserved rest upriver?

Firing above the town continued. The rumbling shook the air, yet it did not sound like a big battle. It was more like a warning of trouble to come.

A stableboy came running with Montcalm's favorite dark bay horse. The general mounted.

A courier came galloping into the camp and drew rein before the general. "The Guyenne Regiment is advancing immediately, sir," he panted. "My commander sent me to advise you that he can see the English on the Plains above Quebec."

"Then it is true!" Montcalm cried. He turned toward his officers as if to reassure them. "There can't be many English—not through a funnel the size of Saint Denis Ravine. But we must capture them at once before they can entrench and open the way for others. There is no time to lose."

He ordered the battalion from the center camp to follow him. He sent a courier for six hundred of the best Canadian and Indian sharpshooters from the left flank.

Then, with Johnstone, Montcalm galloped in the direction of the St. Charles bridge, from which he could see what was going on above the town.

Seconds later Peter heard his troop officer shout, "*Assemblez!*—Fall in!"

He slipped the sling of his drum over his shoulder

and took up his sticks. Like the soldiers around him, he was no longer concerned with hunger or with the wet uniform he wore. His heart beat as fast as his call upon the drum.

All through center camp the drums began to roll. Fifes played and trumpets blared. Over and over Peter beat the call to march, to fight.

The drumming call went on, from drums in every direction, calling the men into action. Soldiers caught up their guns and their bayonets and formed into troops behind their drummers. Officers ran to the front of their ranks, buckling on their swords. Orders were shouted, while the drums kept on warning, urging, "Hurry, hurry!"

"*En avant!*" Peter heard his officer call.

He broke into a march, stepping out boldly before his men. Maybe the hollow feeling in his stomach was fear, but he had not lost the thrill of hearing the sound of boots coming down together behind him. There was a magic in the throb of the drums that made Peter forget himself. He became one with all the soldiers about him, wanting only to follow the loved General Montcalm wherever he might lead. Their general would save Quebec—and New France.

The shooting on the heights above Quebec increased. Urgency rang in the air. Faster, faster, Peter drummed. The men behind him were almost running. Peter saw a troop pass his men. They were completely out of order in their haste and surprise.

His sticks bounced off the drumhead as if in one continuous beat with no time between. He must keep his men together. His legs moved as fast as his drumsticks.

When at length they reached the bridge of boats on the St. Charles the troops halted, waiting as Montcalm rode to meet them. He had been to Vaudreuil's headquarters to talk with the governor. From there he had glimpsed across the valley the red coats of English soldiers on the Heights of Abraham.

He gave one brief order to Captain Johnstone. "Return quickly and command Poulariez to bring the remainder of the left flank to the Plains of Abraham."

Then, without another word, he spurred his horse, galloped over the bridge, and raced across the valley toward the walls of the town.

Drumming madly, Peter kept pace with the battalion of soldiers who followed the general to the Palace Gate. His troop pressed in headlong march through the gate and into the narrow streets of Quebec. Here order broke completely. The soldiers were forced to circle rubble and burned buildings.

The people who earlier had fled in panic from Quebec to the forest and farms were now crowding back inside the walls in desperate fear of the English. Some of them saw Montcalm as he galloped past and rushed forward to hail him.

"*Merci, bon Dieu!* The marquis has come!" they cried. "Montcalm will save us!"

Peter could no longer ply his drumsticks because of the crush of the crowd. Men, women, and children swarmed among the soldiers. They peered into faces, searching for loved husbands or fathers or sons to kiss before the battle.

"The English are at the gates. Save us!"

The pleading voices came from people everywhere, in the streets, on the broken roofs, even on the walls and ramparts where they were gathered to watch the battle they knew was upon them.

Peter felt a quick sharp smarting in his eyes as he brushed past helpless women and children crammed into the town and heard their cries of fear. "We will lose our homes! Oh, France, our dear country! We will all be killed!"

As Peter pushed his way with the troops toward

St. Louis Gate he scanned the faces in the crowds, hoping for a glimpse of Marie. He did not see her, although he knew she must have come back inside the walls to escape the English.

He gained St. Louis Gate, was swept through it, and climbed the slope with men shouldering past him. A part of his mind was alert to hear his officer's command to restore order. Another part remembered the morning he first stood on these Plains of Abraham, the day he had walked in the wilderness to the Indian camp. It seemed years ago rather than only a summer.

Soldiers continued to pour through St. Louis Gate and St. John Gate. They fanned out to form groups and reorganize behind their leaders. With their backs to the walls of Quebec, they faced the Plains.

Peter could not see the enemy. He knew they must be behind the ridge about a mile away, where the firing came from, but there was no way of knowing how many English had climbed the cliffs and were waiting there.

Montcalm lined up the regiments on the Plains much as they were stationed in camp. Peter was in the front center, behind his general. His spine tingled as he watched the rows upon rows of officers and soldiers, in the white and blue uniform of France, lift their gleaming bayonets and cheer as Montcalm rode down their lines.

The fluttering banners of each regiment proclaimed its name: the Royal Roussillon, the Guyenne, the Béarn, the Languedoc, and the La Sarre.

All are gallant men whose enemies have never seen their backs, Peter thought. We have nothing to fear. These men saved Oswego, Carillon, and Fort Henry from the English devils.

But uneasiness persisted as the troops waited in the gray drizzle. In all our past victories we were not taken by surprise, Peter remembered. We knew the position of the enemy and his strength—and had time to plan for battle.

He saw Montcalm order a wing of sharpshooters thrown out on each end of the lines. Indians in scalplock and warpaint and Canadian militia hid in the cornfields and behind pine and cedar trees and among bushes. Others melted into the woods on the right through which ran a road leading to a house where English soldiers had entrenched themselves. The flag of England flew above the house, and the English fired from its windows.

Peter divided his attention between the sharpshooters creeping up on the house held by the

English, and Montcalm, who galloped forward to the ridge to count the enemy.

When Montcalm could see over the ridge he stopped. He was motionless for minutes; then he rode from left to right, as if he were counting a great number of English troops. Peter and the waiting men grew more troubled. The general whirled his horse and drew up before the center in a splatter of mud. The men cheered, then grew quiet as those in front saw their general's white, shocked face. Montcalm's faithful aide-de-camp, Marcel, ran to his side.

"How can it be?" Montcalm exclaimed. "The most we expected was a detachment. Wolfe's whole army is drawn up on the far slope. There must be five thousand English."

Scarcely a sound came from the men as Montcalm sent couriers hurrying away with orders. "Tell Vaudreuil to hurry with his troops to the battlefield," he told one. He sent another to Ramezay, who commanded the garrisons of the town, to ask for the loan of field guns. There was no time to bring cannon from the Beauport camps below the town. The sound of fire from the English beyond the ridge proved that they had hauled small cannon up the path and stationed it in the night.

While the French troops waited—mounted officers with ruffled sleeves in front, subalterns and sergeants along the lines with bayonets set—the firing on the right continued. The Canadians in the woods dodged from tree to tree, raced into the rain of bullets from the English in possession of the house and set fire to it. Several hundred English ran for their lives and rejoined their regiments beyond the ridge. The success of the Canadians brought shouts of victory from the waiting French regulars who cried out eagerly to charge the enemy.

"Let us begin the battle!" the soldiers cried. "Attack the English devils!"

Montcalm rode back and forth before his troops, encouraging them, asking them to be patient.

"Surely Bougainville must hear this fighting," Peter heard the general exclaim. "Why doesn't he come? What is keeping Governor Vaudreuil and his troops?"

Soldiers nearby took up the cry, "Where is Bougainville? He has three thousand of the best soldiers of France. Why doesn't he come from behind the English? We would squeeze the devils then!"

At mid-morning the clouds broke. The sun's beams turned the Plains of Abraham into a dazzle of sparkling light. Peter saw the glitter on swords and wet shrubs and grass. He could not believe that death and destruction waited in this beautiful place.

Montcalm called a council of officers. "We can wait no longer," he told them in a ringing voice that carried down the lines. "If we give the enemy time to improve his position we can never attack him with the few troops we have."

Peter could not hear the answers of the officers. They seemed to agree, although he saw several look toward the woods, as if they hoped Bougainville would appear suddenly with his experienced troops, and toward the town, for Vaudreuil's men.

Montcalm rode in front of his lines, holding his sword high.

"*Vive! Vive le général!*" The shout rose from three thousand throats.

"The time is here!" Montcalm cried. "Here is the battle you have eagerly awaited. Victory must be ours. Retreat means the loss of Quebec—and the loss of the town means the end of New France."

"*Vive! Vive le général!*"

Montcalm whirled and gave the command to advance. The army marched rapidly forward, their banners flying. Peter beat his drum bravely before his men. About him he heard the sounds of many drums and fifes and the war shouts of the soldiers.

The front ranks crested the ridge, then stopped, at the general's command.

Peter looked across the shallow valley. The far slope was red with English soldiers. Three walls of close ranks waited, one behind the other. For a moment Peter's hands ceased to wield the drumsticks as he saw the numbers of the enemy. He had not believed there were so many English in all the New World.

Among the red uniforms he saw a regiment of wild Highlanders, tartans waving and bagpipes screeching. And there nearest the river was the tall English Wolfe leading his grenadiers. Wolfe called to his men. He must be telling them that they face victory or death, Peter thought, and they do. They can never retreat to their ships. The cliff is too steep. They had all night to climb the heights, but we will give them no time to return. We've caught the English in their own trap.

The cheers of the French soldiers showed that they were thinking the same thing.

The French forces behind Peter had reached the ridge now. Montcalm ordered the charge. Drum and fife and trumpet echoed the command through the ranks.

The French charged downhill. Within forty paces of the waiting English, Peter heard the command to fire. The first French volley was too hasty. The Canadians among the troops fell upon the ground to reload. This confused the French regulars, who broke ranks to charge around them.

The English, with superior guns that held two bullets, fired from above as the French came on. Their second volley sounded as one report, like the roar from a cannon.

Half the French first rank fell. Peter saw the two brave commanders of the Sarre and Guyenne Regiments go down. When the short fierce fight ended and the clouds of smoke cleared, the ground was dotted with white- and blue-uniformed men, but the English were unharmed.

The French drew back. Montcalm rode from one point to another, encouraging the men and giving orders.

Higher on the slope, as Wolfe ordered his grenadiers to charge, a bullet struck the English general's wrist. Wolfe wrapped his handkerchief about the wound and called the charge again. His bright red uniform was a perfect target for sharpshooters in the trees. A second bullet struck him. Wolfe staggered but ordered his men on. A third bullet struck his chest, and he fell. He tried to struggle up, as if he did not want his men to know he was hurt. Two officers caught and supported him as he continued to wave the English into battle.

The French charged again. The two armies fired, with their musket muzzles almost touching.

Peter was caught in the mob of men, among roar of guns and rattle of bayonets. The fighting was hand to hand. His drum was torn from his shoulder. Gray-blue smoke from exploding powder swirled about him so that he could no longer see.

He stumbled backward, turned, and did not know the direction he faced. He could hear French and English orders in a confusion of drums and shouts. Shot splattered over him, stinging his cheek. He tasted blood as it ran into the corner of his mouth. He backed against a tree, caught hold of its trunk, and clung a moment.

Which way was the enemy? Where was his own troop?

He heard the fierce yell of the Highlanders from the smoke about him. One of them dashed at Peter with his broadsword.

Peter dodged and stumbled backward over men in white and blue, and men in red, piled on the ground like rows of wheat fallen before a scythe. French soldiers from behind tried to climb over the dead and push forward, only to crumple before English cannon.

Peter realized that the French were falling back. He was carried with them. Cries of dismay rose from the soldiers. They tried again and again to press forward, but the wall of red held relentlessly. French officers ran to and fro, trying to check the retreat. The soldiers themselves struggled to stand and fight, but they were swept back.

In moments, the overthrow of the French regulars was complete. The mass of retreating soldiers caught even Montcalm in their midst and bore him along in their surging torrent. No one could stop. Once Peter was almost trampled under the hoofs of the general's horse. Montcalm shouted orders, but no one could hear them above the stampede of men.

Before the St. Louis Gate, Montcalm managed to draw up his horse. He shouted to the fleeing soldiers, "Turn back! Remember your honor! Remember France! Turn back!"

The sound of his voice finally reached the soldiers nearest him. They rallied about their general. Peter managed to stop among them.

"Hold Quebec," Montcalm cried, "or today New France dies!"

Peter saw Montcalm stiffen suddenly, then sag forward. The general had been struck by a shot from the pursuing English. Soldiers leaped to hold him on his horse. One caught the bridle and began to make a slow way through the pushing masses at the gate of Quebec.

The people of the city, crowded on the walls to watch the battle, recognized their wounded general and began to weep.

"O mon Dieu, le Marquis, it is you!" a woman cried.

Montcalm, seeing the grief in their faces, tried to calm the people. "It is nothing. Do not be troubled for me, my good friends," he managed to say.

But Peter could see that the general was badly hurt. He tried to follow as Montcalm was carried through the gate, but the crowd and the soldiers closed in, blocking the entrance.

Peter saw soldiers running along the wall outside the town to reach the St. Charles River, the bridge, and the comparative safety of the Beauport camps. He ran with them, not knowing what else to do.

The faces of the soldiers who were jogging along beside him were burned and blackened, streaked with perspiration; their mouths were open from shock and strain and breathing on the run.

"Our general, our general—" He heard a soldier weeping. "What can we do without our General Montcalm?"

As Peter passed, he saw Canadian sharpshooters still holding out in the woods on the right. Hidden behind trees, they continued to fight the English step by step. They held the enemy back, making them pay for every inch of ground covered and giving the French regulars time to escape.

When Peter reached the bridge over the St. Charles he saw Governor Vaudreuil coming across it, at last, with his troops. On seeing the retreat, Vaudreuil turned back again.

It was some time after Peter arrived in the right-flank camp beside the St. Charles before he could fully comprehend that he was one of the defeated. He stood and looked at the soldiers, who seemed as stunned as he. For the first time since the enemy fleet arrived in June the French army camps on the Beauport flats were quiet. There was no firing, no bustle of drill or drum, and no singing.

The silence seemed more terrible to Peter than the battle had. He began to tremble. After a time couriers began to arrive from the town, one after another. Their messages were passed along by word of mouth from man to man.

"Wolfe is dead."

"Montcalm is dying."

"The English are afraid to press in to the town after the fleeing French army. . . . The garrisons guarding the walls of Quebec are firing too heavily upon the enemy."

Peter looked at the sun. It was only a little past noon. Yet in these few hours the English were established just outside the walls of Quebec. Without their General Montcalm, the French forces were demoralized. Soldiers were throwing their personal possessions hastily together, preparing to escape.

Peter approached a group of soldiers before their tents. In his hand he held one drumstick which he had clung to, somehow, throughout the battle. A feeling of unreality and amazement still gripped him.

"How did it happen?" he asked the circle of men.

"Bougainville failed us," one answered.

Another cried, "Vaudreuil did not come until the battle was over!"

"Ramezay didn't send help from the town," a third man said. "He kept his troops to guard the ramparts and walls."

Another kept shaking his head. "We had no reserves to push forward when we were exhausted. No one believed we could lose."

"Our luck ran out when Lévis left us," another added.

A tall, thickset soldier spoke angrily. "An army's luck is food and ammunition. That's what we ran out of. Bigot and Cadet defeated France."

"Our General Montcalm fought too soon," another chimed in. "He should have waited until Bougainville and Vaudreuil arrived."

"Montcalm, our poor general," a soldier wept. "We were rallying when he was struck."

Peter tasted tears in the back of his throat. He blinked rapidly. Not one of the soldiers looked up from his fierce concentration on packing blanket and biscuit and powder.

Suddenly Peter thought of Kébec. He must rescue his little dog staked beside his tent at Montcalm's headquarters. Very tired now, Peter slowly walked the long distance to center camp. The soldiers here were scurrying about as frantically as those on the St. Charles.

Kébec barked joyfully when he saw Peter, who caught the puppy in his arms and pressed it against his face. Kébec licked Peter's cheeks. For the first time, Peter felt tears spill and run down his nose.

He sat down before his tent. He was so tired. He had had almost no sleep the night before and little food for days. He lay back on the ground to rest for a few minutes, until some of his own troop might arrive.

He woke with his heart racing to discover that it was growing dark. He sat up but saw no one. The silent, empty tents seemed like a camp for dead men. He could not bear to look toward the dark windows of the stone house that had been filled with activity when Montcalm was there.

Peter wrapped his blanket about Kébec and carried the little dog. As he hurried toward the governor's camp he found a bag containing six hard biscuits that some soldier had dropped. He ate one and fed one to Kébec.

When he reached the St. Charles, he saw in the semidarkness a sea of soldiers milling about. With nothing more than blankets and muskets they were preparing to march, forming into irregular lines. He ran and joined the end of one moving column.

"Are we going to attack again?" he asked those ahead of him.

A soldier turned wearily. "That's all been argued out," he said. "The officers finally voted to retreat toward Montreal. Governor Vaudreuil leads us. He sent a courier ahead to Chevalier de Lévis."

Something in Peter rebelled. He could not bear to

leave the town to the English. But if he stayed, what could he do?

He saw a group of Canadian militiamen break away from the retreating lines and walk toward the town. He ran and caught up with them.

A bearded soldier scowled. "Leave while you can, boy," he said. "We have families in the town. We can't abandon them."

Peter thought of Marie and Grandpère Bonheur, and of Philippe, who was with the town garrison. And surely Colonel Bougainville would come with his troops and Bomazeen. If enough men joined together within the walls, Quebec might still be saved.

"I'm going with you," he said.

XIV. Quebec—French or English?

It was dark when Peter entered the walls through the Palace Gate, the only safe entrance and exit from the town now that the English were camped before the Gates of St. Louis and St. John. He could hear people weeping, and a lump rose in his throat.

Far across the town he saw the glow of torches. He made his way to the crowd of people gathered before the house of the surgeon, Dr. Arnoux. He learned from their hushed conversation that many of the townspeople had been here since General Montcalm was carried into the house after the battle.

"The marquis will yet think of a plan to save us," a woman said.

A militiaman standing beside Peter said that the faithful aide-de-camp, Marcel, was with Montcalm, writing the letters Montcalm dictated and doing what he could for the general's comfort. Commander Ramezay had been to see Montcalm and ask what to do about the town. Couriers had run back and forth from the surgeon's home all afternoon. Most important, a courier had recently gone to the English on the Plains of Abraham with a letter from Montcalm.

Peter's heart beat faster. Did the general believe there was hope of saving Quebec? What had Montcalm written to the English?

A moment later Peter saw Bishop Pontbriand hurry into the surgeon's house. The people grew still.

Kébec, peering from the blanket under Peter's arm, began to whimper, then to bark. Peter hushed the pup and drew aside to the broken wall of a stone house, where he sat on the red and yellow leaves piled there by the wind. Shivering as the night grew colder, he took Kébec upon his lap and wrapped the blanket about them both.

At daybreak Captain Marcel came to the door. His voice broke as he told the people that Montcalm, their beloved general, was dead. Cries and weeping burst from the waiting townspeople.

Peter looked down at his hands a long time. His cheeks grew hot, then cold, and his chest felt as if the shot which killed his general had gone through his own body. He bent forward and held Kébec tightly and let the little dog lick his face.

The people began to leave. Peter stood up and followed them through the streets. He would go to the Bonheurs' home to see if they were safe.

The sun rose, promising a little warmth. He walked a short distance and heard cries of shock and despair from men and women ahead of him. Men stood upon the walls of the town and called to the people below. "The camps are empty. Our army is gone."

A woman cried, "I will not believe it! The army would not desert us!"

Panic gripped the crowd as news spread that the tents were empty in the camps on the Beauport flats.

"The English will destroy us when they discover we have no army to protect us," a woman said, weeping.

"Their rangers will burn us in our homes!" another shrieked.

Men gathered in a knot, discussing, arguing. "We will go to the major," a wounded militiaman said, "and petition for the surrender of Quebec. It is one thing to fight. It is another to see one's family forced to starve and die for no purpose."

"No!" Peter cried from the fringe of the group.

"Winter will yet drive the English home if we hold the town. Montcalm begged us to hold Quebec; for if we don't, it is the end of France in the New World."

No one listened to him.

As Peter approached Marie's house he saw that a corner of it had been torn away by a bomb. The bed in which he had slept was scattered about the garden. The great chest that had held the linens Marie's mother had brought from France lay in splinters. He knew how much Marie loved her home and how she must feel.

He knocked upon the undamaged front door several times. Hearing no answer, he lifted the latch and went in.

By the fireplace sat Grandpère Bonheur with a shawl about his shoulders, his bushy white head sunk forward. Peter spoke to him, but the old man's grief was so great that he did not look up. Peter went quietly past him to the kitchen.

He saw Marie potting a leafy green plant into a small cask of earth upon the kitchen table.

"Peter, thank the good God you are safe!" she cried.

"*Merci beaucoup*, for you the same," he said.

There was a smudge of dirt on the tip of Marie's

nose, but her dark curls were neatly brushed. She looked different—prettier and more grown-up. Suddenly Peter was aware of his own rumpled hair and uniform, of the muddy blanket wrapped about Kébec under his arm. He could think of nothing to say.

Then he saw that Marie was wearing two dresses. Below the full skirt of the new blue dress which Philippe had brought in the package from her aunt in France an inch of the red dress showed. Marie saw him staring.

"We do not know what the day will bring," she explained. "If we must run from the English I'll carry my best dresses away on myself."

Peter couldn't help smiling, but her face was so earnest that he sobered. "Of course," he said. "What is the green stuff you are potting?"

"Parsley," she answered. "A bomb tore up our garden, but parsley roots are hard to kill. I brought this in for the winter—one must have parsley for good soup." With her hands about the greens, her voice faltered. "Peter, do you think Quebec will fall? Excuse me—I guess I'm not very brave."

Peter looked at her, trying to save her best dresses, potting parsley for the winter's soup, and he knew that no matter what happened to Quebec, Marie

would go on making the kind of home her mother
had taught her to make, with as much order and
beauty as she could bring to it.

"You are *very* brave, Marie," he said.

Kébec, who had been quiet a long time for him,
struggled in the blanket and yelped. Marie ran and
took the pup and petted him. "He is hungry," she
said to Peter, "and we have nothing to eat."

Peter took the four remaining biscuits from his
pocket and gave one to each of them: Marie, Kébec,
and himself. He saved the last for Grandpère Bonheur. When he had eaten his biscuit he was as hungry
as before. "We have to have food," he said. "Maybe
I can find some berries and roots in the woods."

Marie shook her head. "The women and children
have cleaned the fields and woods of berries and roots
which can be eaten. We must think of something
else."

"We could fish," Peter said, "if we had lines and
hooks."

Marie's face lighted. "Grandpère used to have
some." She ran into another room and came back
with several hand lines attached to fishhooks, also
a hatchet.

"We must have wood too, for a fire," she said.

She told her grandfather that they would be back soon and that he could keep Kébec for company. Still the old man seemed not to hear.

"I am sorry your *grandpère* is so stricken by our defeat," Peter said as they left the house.

Marie turned suddenly. "Peter," she said. "I will *not* starve. I will *not* let my *grandpère* be hungry. I will *not*."

In the meadow on their way to the St. Charles River, Peter caught a frog which they used for bait. After an hour Marie hooked a silvery fish as long as her forearm, but Peter's line and bobber didn't sink once.

"Never mind," Marie said as they carried home the fish and the wood Peter had cut. "My fish is such a beauty, he'll be more than we can eat tonight."

Maybe Marie does not mean to sound smug, Peter thought, but tomorrow I will fish again until I catch one at least as big!

When they reached the Bonheur home Peter built a fire in the kitchen fireplace while Marie prepared the fish for cooking. "I wish Philippe could eat with us," she said. "He loves baked fish."

"I will try to find him," Peter said.

It was growing dark as Peter crossed the town. He turned a corner and came upon a throng of mourning people who moved slowly behind a gun-cart that held a long box draped with the white flag of France. Many of the men carried torches to light the way. Peter snatched off his cap and stood at attention as the gun-cart rumbled by. This could be no less than his general's, the Marquis de Montcalm's, funeral procession. Peter followed it to the Ursuline chapel.

While men carried the coffin into the chapel Peter stopped and stood with many others for whom there was no room within.

He saw an old soldier wipe his eyes with the back of his hand and heard him say to another, "They dug the bomb crater a little deeper and will lay our general there before the altar."

That must be the bomb crater I saw beneath the railing when Marie and I knelt there before fleeing Quebec, Peter thought.

Peter heard the voice of Abbé Resche, the *curé* of Quebec, chant the *Libera*, and the response of several nuns. He bowed his head as he saw others bare theirs.

In the chapel were the high officials of the church and the town, and the few officers of the army who remained to honor Montcalm. Outside, Peter stood among militiamen in tattered uniforms, coureurs de bois and Indian chiefs, farmers and ragged children, merchants, sailors, voyageurs, old women with shawls about their heads, and young pretty girls with solemn faces.

When Montcalm had been carried through the gate after the battle, cries of grief and surprise filled the air. Now there was only wordless sorrow, as if this hurt was too deep for crying.

Now you will never see home again, my general, Peter thought, but as long as one person lives in Quebec, you will be loved and honored.

As the crowd broke up and people moved away into the darkness, weeping began. "This is the death of France," Peter heard a man say, but he refused to believe that.

He felt that Philippe must be here some place, but the darkness hid him. Peter knew that the fish would be cooked and that Marie would be worrying. He returned to the house.

While they ate the delicious fish Peter told Marie and her grandfather about Montcalm's funeral. He had scarcely finished his story when Major Joannes came into the house and said that he was on his way home from a meeting of a council called by Ramezay.

The major waited for Grandpère Bonheur to show

that he had heard. The old man raised his head at last.

"It has come?" he asked. These were the first words he had spoken since the battle.

"The officers of the corps, all but one, believe we should surrender Quebec," the major answered.

"The one must be Fiedmont," Grandpère Bonheur said slowly. "Our brave commander of the town artillery would never give up."

"Nor I," Major Joannes said brokenly. "But Ramezay read us written orders sent by Vaudreuil before the governor left the Beauport camps. Vaudreuil ordered us to surrender rather than let the town be destroyed, for there is no shelter for the people any place and winter is here. We have in the garrison less than a week's supply of food at half-rations."

"I would rather freeze and starve," the old man said.

"And I," Major Joannes replied. "But the people who came into the town increased our population to six thousand. Almost half of these are women and children. Another thousand are wounded and sick soldiers. We have only fifteen hundred militiamen and sailors, and six hundred regulars. What are these against the whole English army and their fleet?"

"You did not talk so the day I ran away from La Friponne!" Peter cried hotly. He was sorry as soon as he saw the pain in Major Joannes's eyes.

"We could hope then," the major said.

During the next several days cold torrents of rain kept everyone indoors or huddled in such shelter as could be found. Outside the walls the enemy advanced toward the St. Louis Gate and began to build a redoubt. The town's artillery captain, Fiedmont, erected batteries overlooking the heights and fired upon the English, continually making breeches in their construction. The French batteries at the mouth of the St. Lawrence River kept at bay the English fleets in the harbor.

About noon on the eighteenth of September Major Joannes came to the house through the storm. He put his arm about Grandpère Bonheur's shoulder and almost wept with joy.

"We have new hope," he said. "Bougainville sent a courier. He is camped with his army at Cap-Rouge. He had received a letter from Vaudreuil saying that Lévis met the army at Jacques Cartier River and all are heartened by Lévis' presence and plans."

"Who was the courier?" Peter cried.

Major Joannes seemed not to hear him. "Bougainville says he is sending the cavalry with bags of biscuits—one hundred horsemen with biscuit. He promises they will arrive without fail. This changes everything. Now we shall have food."

Marie came from the kitchen with Kébec at her heels. Peter saw how much she loved the little dog, and Kébec followed her everywhere.

"Bougainville is sending biscuits," Peter said to her.

Major Joannes explained to Grandpère Bonheur. "The cavalry will cut through the woods, ford the River Saint Charles at low tide, and enter the town by the Palace Gate."

"Who was the courier?" Peter asked again.

"An Indian boy," Major Joannes answered.

"Bomazeen!" Peter said. "Where is he?"

But Major Joannes was too full of excitement to hear anything but his own words to Grandpère Bonheur. "An hour ago Ramezay ordered me to raise the surrender flag on the ramparts and go to the English with offers of capitulation, but I would not. I think I have convinced him. If we can only hold out until the biscuits come, and if Bougainville and Lévis return with their armies—"

Now Peter's excitement was as great as the major's. He wanted to know how much more Bomazeen knew. Quebec might still be saved for France.

"Where is Bomazeen?" he asked again.

"Waiting at the garrison," Major Joannes said, "to take back Ramezay's reply—when the final word is said."

Peter ran from the house into the storm to find his friend.

There were many garrisons and no one seemed to know where Commander Ramezay was at the moment. Several hours passed before Peter came upon Bomazeen, sitting alone in a small entry before a closed door. The two greeted each other joyfully. The sound of men's voices, indignant, reached them from the room beyond.

"They quarrel," Bomazeen said. "Ramezay insists on surrender. Fiedmont says no."

"What do you think?" Peter asked.

Bomazeen answered gravely. "I think our brother from across the water has fallen on his face and will not rise again."

Peter's hopes fell. "Does Colonel Bougainville believe this?" he asked.

"I do not know," Bomazeen said. "How can he know what conditions are in the town? The day of the battle we reached the Plains too late. We crept to the edge of the woods, but the army had fled and we could not attack alone."

"Did Colonel Bougainville think the Guyenne Regiment was on the Plains that night, and stay at Cap-Rouge?" Peter asked.

Bomazeen nodded. "Bougainville was sending the supply barges downriver. He thought less suspicion would be aroused if we did not follow them."

Peter felt a bitter taste in his mouth. "I hate Bigot —all La Friponne," he said. "If they had not cheated and stolen we would have had supplies enough. Bigot and the Grand Company are more to blame than the English if we lose Quebec. I cannot bear that they live and go free, while Montcalm is dead and cannot accuse them."

"They will not escape," Bomazeen said quietly. "Remember the day Colonel Bougainville and I were at center camp to see the general?"

"*Oui*," Peter said, and thought, a little more than a week in time, years in trouble.

"Our general had a feeling, I think," Bomazeen said. "Anyway, he gave us two packets of accusations written in his own hand, with records of the wrongs committed by La Friponne against the people and the army. These packets are safely hidden in the

Abnaki camp. They will reach France when ships sail again."

The closed door behind Peter was thrown open violently. Captain Fiedmont stood on the threshold. He turned and shouted at someone in the room. "Quebec is not lost—as long as her walls stand and my powder lasts!"

"Then what? When the powder is gone?" Peter heard a tired voice ask. Commander Ramezay came from the room and faced Captain Fiedmont. In his hand he held a paper. "These are the terms of surrender. Major Joannes will take them to the English. I have already ordered the flag of surrender to be raised on both the land and water sides of town."

"But it is only four o'clock and the English gave us until eleven tonight before they will attack the town," Fiedmont argued. "Something may yet—"

"Such things take time," Ramezay interrupted. "Look, there above the wall, the surrender flag is already going up."

Peter felt grief like a knife thrust between his ribs. Bomazeen too was silent.

"Ramezay could have waited until the biscuit arrived," Peter said. "There must be some way."

"General Montcalm did not think so," Bomazeen said quietly.

"Montcalm?" Peter said. "How do you know?"

"A courier brought Colonel Bougainville a copy of our general's letter written to the English as he lay dying."

Peter looked at Bomazeen.

"Our general begged Monsieurs Townshend and Murray, who took command after the English Wolfe's death, to show the well-known humanity of the English to all French and Canadian prisoners."

Then Montcalm had believed Quebec lost before he died. What pain for the proud general!

Peter and Bomazeen heard a commotion and came out of the garrison. At the city wall they saw a struggle among several soldiers who were standing beneath the flag of surrender. Peter recognized Major Joannes, who was fighting to get free of two soldiers ordered to hold him. Joannes climbed the wall and tore down the flag of surrender and crushed it in his hands.

Peter's throat tightened. He could no longer look upon Major Joannes's frenzy. He turned and walked into the street with Bomazeen.

At eleven that night Peter stood among the silent throng of townspeople and watched Major Joannes obey Ramezay's order to walk through the St. Louis

Gate and hand over the signed papers of surrender to the English. As the major left the torchlighted gate and entered the strip of darkness between the town and the English entrenchment, cries broke out in the streets of Quebec. The crowd of people behind Ramezay took up the words. Peter found himself shouting.

"The cavalry! Our cavalry is coming in through the Palace Gate with the biscuits!"

Men and women wept openly as the soldiers drew up their tired horses before Ramezay. Peter saw that the cavalrymen and horses were glistening wet from fording rivers and their long ride through the darkness and rain. Even the bags of biscuits slung over the saddle dripped water.

Ramezay looked into the faces of the exhausted cavalrymen, and he could not speak.

"We are too late?" the leader of the cavalry asked.

Ramezay nodded. "Tomorrow the gates of Quebec open to the English."

For a long breath, Peter's heart seemed to stop beating. He heard no sound in all the town. It seemed that the very waters of the St. Lawrence stood still at Ramezay's words.

In the darkness over the heads of the stunned people a murmur rose, like a cry from the ghosts of all the men of France who had struggled and died through a hundred and fifty years to make and hold a place in the New World. Peter felt he could hear Champlain, Cartier, Marquette, and stern old Frontenac.

The cavalrymen lifted the bags of biscuit and dropped them on the ground, then turned their horses and left as they had come, before they too could be captured with the town. Wordlessly, the starving people stooped to pick up the food.

The next morning Peter saw that the storm was past. The sun shone upon him as he joined the people who stood in the streets and discussed the terms of capitulation agreed upon.

In hushed voices people told one another that the garrison was to have the honors of war, to march out of the town with arms and baggage to the beat of their drums. All French soldiers would be returned to France on English ships. The Canadian people were not to be punished for fighting in defense of their homes. Their property was to belong to them and they were granted freedom of religion.

XV. Peter's Choice

On the nineteenth, in the late afternoon, Peter saw
the gates of Quebec opened. A staff of English officers on horseback entered, followed by a field gun
bearing the English flag. Behind them marched grenadiers and artillery. The English crossed the town and
stopped before the Château St. Louis.

Peter followed with Bomazeen and Marie and stood
in the crowd of people near the edge of the terrace
above the Lower Town. Philippe joined them as
Ramezay handed the keys of the Palace to the English commander, General Townshend.

The white-uniformed officers of France, on guard
for the last time, stepped back and gave their places
to the red-coated English. On Mountain Hill the
white flag of France fluttered down. The flag of
England rose in its place, greeted by a roar of English cannon from the fleet in the harbor.

Peter pretended not to see the tears rolling down
Marie's cheeks or the muscle jumping in Philippe's
throat. He didn't even move to wipe the tears which
fell from his own chin.

When it seemed that he could bear the sight no
longer, Marie said, "One must always eat. You will
come home with us, Philippe and Bomazeen?"

In the Bonheur living room, where they gathered,
logs blazed in the fireplace and the round dining table
gleamed with a high polish. It seemed to Peter that
the house was almost as pleasant as the day he had
arrived in Quebec and come here with Philippe—
if one could forget the ruined walls which lay behind the closed door of the corner bedroom.

"Where is your *grandpère?*" he asked Marie.

"He will not rise from his bed," Marie said. "Today, for him, France died."

Peter nodded. "I did not know until it happened
that defeat could hurt so much."

Marie turned quickly toward the kitchen. Peter

followed and helped her bring baked fish and place it upon the table. There was a ration of biscuit from the cavalry and flat corn cakes that Marie had made from Indian meal which Bomazeen had brought with him.

While they sat about the table Peter said, *"C'est fini.* We must make plans."

"Will you stay in Quebec?" Marie asked.

"Not even this night under English rule," Peter answered. Then, seeing the look in her eyes, he hastened to add, "Quebec is your home, Marie, but it is not mine."

"Then where do you call home?" Philippe asked.

Peter puckered his dark brows. "Truly, I do not know," he said. "Once I would have said France. Now . . ."

"You know that if you want to return to France the English ships will transport you free, since you are with the army?" Philippe said.

"Oui," Peter replied thoughtfully. "I love France, but there is no opportunity as long as the selfish king spends twice as much as the people can earn."

"I know," Philippe said.

"What are *you* going to do, Philippe?" Marie asked.

"I leave tonight for the far-north country," he

said. "My coureurs de bois and I have bateaux at the Indian village. We will trap all winter. Surely the English will pay better prices for furs than La Friponne."

"I want to trap furs," Peter said. "I have been thinking again of furs since I knew the town was lost. Let me go with you."

"When you are older and more experienced in wilderness ways," Philippe said. "The far north is no place for a boy." Peter looked down at his plate and tried to hide his deep disappointment. "But I am glad that you want to remain in the New World," Philippe said. "I told you once that this war was fought for furs and land—remember?"

Peter nodded.

"The furs and the land are still here," Philippe said. "This great country of America remains wide and free even under English rule. No matter which king claims it, the land will belong to the people who settle it—that means you and me—as well as to the English, Peter."

Peter blinked. Philippe felt as sad as he did about the loss of the New World to France, yet Philippe spoke of making a permanent home here.

"The first lesson the wilderness teaches," Philippe said gently, "is that one cannot always win. We must make the best of defeat, Peter, and begin again."

Peter looked up and tried to smile. Bomazeen was watching him.

"I will trap this winter on the land of my people at Lake Champlain," Bomazeen said. "Will you come with me, Peter?"

Philippe's face lighted. "Lake Champlain!" he said. "There is a beautiful wilderness, and it has belonged to France for a hundred and fifty years—since Champlain discovered the lake."

Bomazeen's chin lifted. "I do not know when Champlain saw it," he said, "but the peaceful lake has belonged to *my* people since the beginning of the world."

The young Abnaki turned to Peter. "I chose you— the day I found you standing in the river, scowling and scrubbing your clothes. I call you now by the name of my people, my *nioba*, he who shall be to me more than a brother. Come with me, Peter, and my country shall be your country."

Peter was so moved he did not know what to say.

"Don't go, Peter," Marie begged. "The Mohawk Indians, who fought with the English, also claim the land about Champlain. You'll be killed."

"The English-loving Mohawks never belonged on

Lake Champlain," Bomazeen said scornfully. "They only *hope* to hunt there."

"You see?" Marie insisted. "There will be fighting among the Mohawks and the Abnaki'."

Bomazeen turned to her. "Do not worry. On the little Isle la Motte in the lake is a sanctuary, a truce place respected by Mohawk and Abnaki alike. Peter and I will build a log cabin not far from this place of safety."

Peter's heart beat hard. The Abbé had told him first about the New World, but he had discovered much more for himself. Here was adventure, wilderness to explore, furs to trap. He remembered the furs which the coureurs de bois had spilled onto the table in the intendant's kitchen, how glossy and soft to his touch they were. And in the council of chiefs, redmen had spoken their thoughts openly and voted what they would do. Here was freedom which the Old World never offered, and here was land to earn for one's own. For these blessings he would risk much danger.

"I will go," Peter said. "We will be *niobas*, Bomazeen."

They pushed back their chairs from the table, making ready to leave. Peter saw that Marie remained seated. Her lips trembled. Kébec lay at her feet and whined sympathetically.

Marie had been so kind to Peter. He wished that he could do something for her.

He saw Marie reach down and lift the pup to her lap and stroke its ears. His heart skipped a beat. No, he could not give Kébec to anyone. His dog was all he had. But he waited. He could not take the pup while it licked Marie's cheek.

Philippe stopped before Marie. "*Merci, chérie,* this is the first good dinner I have had since I was here last," he said. "Remember me to your grandfather when he feels better—and he will, I know. I'll see you in the spring."

"*Merci beaucoup,*" Marie said. Peter saw that she could not say any more.

Bomazeen thanked her and went to the door with Philippe. Peter stood alone.

"Good-by, Peter," she said. "May *le bon Dieu* go with you."

She placed the squirming Kébec in Peter's arms. Peter held the pup tight for a moment and swallowed. Then he thrust Kébec back at Marie so she had to catch the pup to keep it from falling.

"Kébec is yours," Peter said. "I have no place to keep him."

Such a radiant smile broke over Marie's face that Peter's heart lifted.

"I will keep Kébec for you—until you return in the spring with your furs," she promised.

With Bomazeen, Peter crossed the dark town, left through Palace Gate, walked through the valley of the St. Charles, and entered the wilderness. Silently he followed the Indian along a trail Bomazeen knew well even at night.

Peter felt again the excitement of the wilderness. Here was the remembered fragrance of pine and spruce. Again he heard the wind like a harp in the branches above him. The forest's freedom and peace moved through him, and he smiled.

It is as Philippe said, he told himself. There is room for all in this new America. I believe I chose well.

Epilogue: The Aftermath

The battle on the Plains of Abraham was one of the great decisive battles of all time. With the threat of French domination ended in Canada, the American colonists turned their attention to gaining independence from all rule from across the Atlantic. Seventeen years later many French soldiers who remained in the New World, as Peter did, fought with the Americans for independence and became American citizens. Others remained as settlers in Canada.

The real Peter Demo, the author's great-great-great-grandfather (whose name is believed to have been originally spelled de Mont, then DeMont, and finally Anglicized to Demo), roamed the wilderness for several years with the Abnaki' and the coureurs de bois, became a fur-trader in Quebec, married, lived for a time on the shore of the St. Lawrence in what is now New York State, and finally settled on the Grand Isle in Lake Champlain—near the present location of North Hero, Vermont. He lived to be one hundred and twelve years old and died in the year of the hundredth anniversary of the fall of Quebec.

When Bigot and Cadet and other members of the Grand Company of Associates returned to France, they were seized and imprisoned in the Bastille. Brought to trial, they denied the many charges of stealing and fraud against their own country. When confronted with positive evidence, each testified against the other to save himself. Bigot was banished from France for life, his property was confiscated, and he paid a heavy fine. Cadet was forced to pay back six million francs and was banished from Paris for nine years. Other members of the Grand Company of Associates were sentenced to various fines and held in prison until these were paid.

True Events of the Siege of Quebec

Summer 1759

Late May Bougainville returns from France to Quebec with twenty-three ships. These carry a bare third of the supplies requested by Montcalm and only a handful of recruits for the army. But Bougainville brings a message that a great English fleet is known to be ready to sail against Quebec—under command of General Wolfe.

June 26 The English fleet arrives and anchors off the Isle d'Orléans.

June 28 The French send fire rafts against the English ships.

June 29 The English First Army occupies the Isle d'Orléans, opposite the Montmorency Falls.

July 2 The English Second Army occupies Point Lévis on the St. Lawrence River directly opposite the town of Quebec. They begin to bombard the town with cannon.

July 9 The English First Army occupies the left bank of the Montmorency River, the opposite bank already being held by the French under Chevalier François de Lévis.

July 18 On this dark night several English ships succeed in passing the French batteries on the St. Lawrence and arrive safely above the town.

July 19 Montcalm sends Bougainville with experienced troops to keep constant watch along the north shore of the St. Lawrence and prevent any English landing.

July 26 Wolfe leads the English First Army along the left bank of the Montmorency, hoping to find a ford and attack the French camps. He is thrown back by Lévis' soldiers from Montreal and by the Indians and Canadians.

Month of August Continued bombardment of the town from Point Lévis. More and more English ships evade the French batteries and join Admiral Holmes's ships above the town. Their force threatens supplies from Montreal and Three Rivers—even threatens Montreal itself.

August 9 Chevalier de Lévis and troops of Montreal soldiers return to that city, leaving Montcalm and Vaudreuil in charge at Quebec. Bougainville's troops are exhausted with long marches and counter-marches on the north shore and with several encounters when they repulse the English attempts to land.

August 31–September 3 The English army breaks camp and leaves the Montmorency River. Great rejoicing follows in the French camps as they see the English preparing to leave before the winter.

September 12 At night Admiral Saunders' group of English ships in Quebec Harbor shows great activity, as if preparing to attack the French camps. Fear is felt for supply barges which Bougainville is sending down-river in the night.

September 13 Battle of the Plains of Abraham: Wolfe is killed; Montcalm is mortally wounded. Vaudreuil flees with the French army toward Montreal.

September 14   Montcalm dies and is buried that evening in the Ursuline chapel.

September 18   Ramezay surrenders Quebec to the English.

September 19   The English march into Quebec and raise the flag of England on Mountain Hill and the Citadel.